Escape to beautiful Tuscany and Lake Como in this romantic new duet

One Summer in Italy

From Harlequin Romance author
Michelle Douglas

Frankie Weaver and Audrey Dimarco are cousins in Australia, and when their late grandmother leaves them a bequest to spend the summer in Italy, they can't wait to start their travels!

Frankie has big decisions to make about her future, while Audrey has new family members to meet near Lake Como...but both find their Italian escapades result in romantic encounters that could change all their plans!

Book 1: *Unbuttoning the Tuscan Tycoon*

Book 2: *Cinderella's Secret Fling*

Both available now!

D1048015

Dear Reader,

I'm so excited for you to read the second book in my One Summer in Italy duet. In this book, Audrey finds herself living a dream come true in gloriously gorgeous Lake Como.

Who of us hasn't secretly dreamed of being gifted a windfall, of being whisked into a world of wealth and glamour where suddenly anything is possible? Having a chance to wear designer gowns, sip expensive French champagne while living in an eighty-room lakefront mansion. It's what happens to Audrey, though the real prize is the discovery of the family she never knew she had.

The only blemish in this otherwise glorious existence is the forbidding Gabriel Dimarco, the father of her sweet four-year-old niece. Gabriel is disapproving not only of this new world she finds herself in, but of her new family, too. Gabriel has been badly burned by an heiress before and has absolutely no intention of falling for the bewitching Audrey. Forced to spend the summer together, however, they discover hidden depths in each other and in themselves, too.

Cinderella's Secret Fling is a story of hope and forgiveness and new starts, and I hope you love it as much as I do.

Hugs,

Michelle

Cinderella's Secret Fling

—

Michelle Douglas

Recycling programs
for this product may
not exist in your area.

ISBN-13: 978-1-335-73717-5

Cinderella's Secret Fling

Copyright © 2023 by Michelle Douglas

For questions and comments about the quality of this book,
please contact us at CustomerService@Harlequin.com.

Harlequin Enterprises ULC
22 Adelaide St. West, 41st Floor
Toronto, Ontario M5H 4E3, Canada
www.Harlequin.com

Printed in U.S.A.

Michelle Douglas has been writing for Harlequin since 2007 and believes she has the best job in the world. She lives in a leafy suburb of Newcastle, on Australia's east coast, with her own romantic hero, a house full of dust and books, and an eclectic collection of '60s and '70s vinyl. She loves to hear from readers and can be contacted via her website, michelle-douglas.com.

Books by Michelle Douglas

Harlequin Romance

One Summer in Italy

Unbuttoning the Tuscan Tycoon

Redemption of the Maverick Millionaire
Singapore Fling with the Millionaire
Secret Billionaire on Her Doorstep
Billionaire's Road Trip to Forever
Cinderella and the Brooding Billionaire
Escape with Her Greek Tycoon
Wedding Date in Malaysia
Reclusive Millionaire's Mistletoe Miracle

Visit the Author Profile page
at Harlequin.com for more titles.

To Trisha Pender for her enthusiasm, support and a shared love of the romance genre.

Praise for
Michelle Douglas

"Michelle Douglas writes the most beautiful stories, with heroes and heroines who are real and so easy to get to know and love.... This is a moving and wonderful story that left me feeling fabulous.... I do highly recommend this one, Ms. Douglas has never disappointed me with her stories."

—*Goodreads* on *Redemption of the Maverick Millionaire*

PROLOGUE

My darling Audrey,
I know this is going to come as a great shock
to you, and I'm hoping you do not blame
me too much for not revealing this to you
sooner, but I know how much family means
to you. And this is not a secret I can take to
the grave. The decision for how to proceed
is yours, my dearest girl—not mine, not your
father's and certainly not your mother's.

My mother? I can almost hear you ask.
Yes. She is not who she claimed to be and I
have discovered her true identity. I'm sorry
to tell you she passed away many years ago,
and it was a brief news item reporting her
death that prompted my suspicions and sub-
sequent investigations.

Rather than being a poor orphan, as she
always claimed, she came from a very old,
very powerful and very wealthy Italian fam-
ily. And apparently, you have an Italian
grandmother and a plethora of cousins.

Your aunt Beatrice is now in possession
of all the associated documentation, and
she has been in contact with your maternal
grandmother's lawyers. Your grandmother's
name is Marguerite Funaro, and she wishes
to meet you. If you wish to meet her, you can
now do so. The choice is yours.

*Wishing you all joy and every happiness
and a life filled with love and family.
Your ever-loving Nonna*

AUDREY STARED AT the letter in her hand and then
up at her aunt Beatrice. *Aunt* was an honorary
title, but Nonna's best friend had always felt like
family. For the past month she'd been in Lake
Como staying with Aunt Beatrice, and yet all this
time she'd had a family she'd never known about?
'This says…'

'Yes.' Beatrice nodded.

'I have…?'

'A family? *Si*, Audrey, it would appear so. Your
grandmother wanted me to make contact with them
first as she did not want you getting your hopes up
if they did not wish to recognise you. On the contrary, though, they very much want to meet you.'

A champagne fizz of excitement bubbled in her
chest. And something deeper. Something that made
her catch her breath.

If she was being brutally honest—and she was
always brutally honest, at least with herself—she'd
not fully regained her balance since Johanna had
died. Losing a twin… It felt as if she'd lost a part
of herself.

She'd been finding her feet again, though,
slowly, every step hard-won. Then her father had
made the shocking announcement that he was

marrying and relocating to America. She hadn't even known he'd been seeing someone!

Then Nonna had died. Her throat thickened. She doubted anything could fill the gap that now yawned through her. It took a superhuman effort to swallow the lump stretching her throat into a painful ache. Her family, never large, had suddenly dwindled to her, her cousin Frankie and her aunt Deidre.

But to now discover her mother's family... *A grandmother and a plethora of cousins.* She'd been searching for something to anchor her, a safe harbour. Could this be it?

'Would you like to meet them?'

It felt as if the sun had come from behind a cloud and bathed her in light. A big extended family? She clasped her hands in her lap. She wanted that more than she'd ever wanted anything. 'Yes, please. How soon can it be arranged?'

CHAPTER ONE

'YOU ARE READY, AUDREY?'

The words sounded more like a command than a question. Audrey glanced at her grandmother and found she couldn't push a single word from a throat that had grown too tight. She'd met Marguerite Funaro a week ago, and Marguerite was as unlike Nonna as it was possible to be.

'Appearances can be deceptive.'

She held that thought close; the voice—Nonna's—made the tight knot in her stomach loosen a fraction. Nonna had taught her the importance of family. Audrey had no intention of forgetting those lessons and abandoning all of Nonna's wisdom now, just because she was nervous and things felt a bit awkward.

Marguerite might not be touchy-feely and demonstrative, but Audrey had felt a bond with the older woman the moment they'd met. Marguerite hadn't felt like a stranger, although the world she inhabited did.

In her letter, Nonna had said Audrey's mother's family was wealthy and powerful. Audrey just hadn't realised how wealthy and powerful. Apparently, the Funaro name was synonymous with all the great aristocratic names of Italy.

She pinched herself. It was hard to believe that *she* was a member of such an old, powerful Italian family. Or that she was now a resident at their impossibly luxurious estate on the shores of Lake Como with its splendid Funaro Villa, extravagant gardens and extraordinary views.

She glanced at her grandmother again and her stomach churned. She didn't want to let Marguerite down. Didn't want to let any of the family down, but what did she know about this world? How would she ever fit in?

Just because Marguerite is regal and proud, it doesn't mean she has no heart or kindness or love.

The thought made her straighten. Marguerite had welcomed her into the Funaro fold without hesitation…and with her own brand of warmth. Lifting her chin, she nodded. 'I'm looking forward to meeting the rest of the family, Grandmother.'

Grandmother was what Marguerite had requested Audrey call her. She had no idea why she wanted her to use the English title rather than the Italian one. Maybe it was so she could tell her apart from the other members of the family.

Because, apparently, there were quite a few of them.

The wriggle of delight was cut short as Marguerite's gaze roved over Audrey's attire. Her lips didn't tighten and her nostrils didn't flare and nothing about her face gave anything away, but Audrey couldn't help but feel she'd been found wanting.

She glanced down at herself. 'Would you like me to change?' Not that she had anything else to change into. Not really. 'I only brought a limited wardrobe with me on this trip.' She only had a limited wardrobe period, but she had no intention of admitting that out loud. 'I've not had a chance to do any real shopping yet and—'

'Audrey!'

She snapped to attention. 'Yes, Grandmother?'

'You are a granddaughter of the Funaro family. You have royal blood flowing in your veins.'

She choked down an entirely inappropriate laugh. Royal blood? *Her?*

'Your attire does not define you.'

Easy to say when you happened to be wearing a delightfully chic Chanel suit in pink-and-white tweed.

'You will walk out there as if you own the room.'

Oh, just like that, huh? Easy-peasy. She had an insane urge to call her cousin Frankie and demand a pep talk.

'You will keep your back straight, your chin high and a pleasant expression on your face.'

She adjusted her stance to meet her grandmother's exacting requirements.

'Ours is a large family and, as with most families, some members get along better than others. You will not allow anyone to ruffle your peace or to allow you to feel inferior.'

Okay, now she really wanted to run back to Aunt Beatrice's and hide under the bed that had been hers for the past few weeks.

'Repeat that, please,' the older woman ordered.

'I won't allow anyone to make me feel inferior,' she obediently repeated. These people were her family; things were bound to be a bit awkward initially. But it wasn't money and position that made a person worthwhile. Just because her dress wasn't the latest fashion, it didn't make her a bad person.

Her heart beat hard. She had family. And she *would* fit in. It might take some time, but she *would* make them love her. There was strength in family, not to mention security. And a place to belong. Ever since Nonna's death, she'd felt cast adrift. But here was a place where she could find safe harbour and acceptance—where she could love and be loved.

'Remember, you have your grandmother's seal of approval.'

Marguerite might not be all touchy-feely maternal warmth, but her unerring support warmed Audrey from the inside out. 'I'm ready to meet everyone, Grandmother. I'm looking forward to it.'

Once this initial meeting was over, she could work at getting to know everyone on a more leisurely and less formal basis. She imagined lunches, dinners, outings. Hopefully by Christmas it'd feel as if they'd all known each other forever. She crossed her fingers.

'Remember, spine straight, shoulders back… and smile.'

Audrey followed the instructions to the letter, and then waited outside a set of gilded double doors while a butler or footman or…well, a member of staff who wore the most extraordinary uniform, flung the doors open. She half expected him to announce them.

He didn't, of course. This wasn't the set of a historical drama. She wasn't some Jane Austen heroine. This was the real world.

Except Audrey's real world wasn't Lake Como, glittering chandeliers, eighty-room villas and *a new family*.

Marguerite took Audrey's arm, as if for the support—as if she was an old lady who needed to lean on someone. Which was a joke, because *frailty, thy name is woman* wasn't Marguerite. She doubted she'd be able to best the older woman in an arm wrestle.

The thought, though, made her smile.

Then they stepped inside the room and her breath caught. There had to be at least forty people in here. It took all her strength not to clasp her hands beneath her chin and beam at them. How *wonderful*! She'd always wanted to be part of a big, loving family.

Nobody said a word as she and Marguerite split a path through the crowd towards a throne—

Not a throne. A chair. But it was all gold gilt

and pink velvet and clearly Marguerite's. The silence raised all the fine hairs on her arms. She concentrated on keeping her spine straight, her chin lifted and her expression pleasant. This odd formality must be the way they did things here in her new world.

Still, she'd never hated her height more. It always made her stand out, gave her nowhere to hide and— Except…she wasn't the only tall person in the room! This stature must be a Funaro trait. Her smile widened. Surely, that meant she was fitting in already.

Marguerite removed her arm from Audrey's and sat. Audrey immediately felt cast adrift.

Don't be a baby.

It'd be easier if she knew what she was supposed to do. Should she sit? Except there was no chair beside her grandmother's.

You're not supposed to sit. You're supposed to mix and mingle and get to know everyone.

Not until she'd been introduced, though, surely? She felt as if she ought to have a sign around her neck saying Exhibit A.

The vision had her lips twitching. Once everyone got to know her, she wouldn't be such a curiosity. She'd be just another member of the family.

And still, the silence stretched. Though, she couldn't help feeling an awful lot of silent communication was happening among various family members. She hid a wince. Awkward much?

Finally, with an impatient huff, a child broke from the ranks and came hurtling out from behind the crowd to rush up to Audrey, hopping from one foot to the other in front of her. '*Ciao!* Hello!'

The pretty little thing couldn't be older than three or four. Something inside her melted. She hadn't thought, but of course, there'd be children. She knelt down to be eye to eye with her and held out her hand. 'I'm Audrey. And who might you be? A princess, maybe?'

'I'm not a princess. I'm Liliana.' She placed her hand in Audrey's and shook it earnestly. 'And you're my aunty.'

She stared at the little girl and her throat thickened; her eyes burned. She had a niece? She had to swallow before she could trust her voice to work. 'My niece? I have a niece?'

Little Liliana nodded eagerly.

The delight that flooded her couldn't be hidden, contained or otherwise tempered. She clapped her hands, grinning madly. She might've even shimmied. 'That is the best news I've ever heard!'

She had a niece!

Liliana grinned back like she couldn't help it, either.

And then they hugged each other like they meant it.

She had at least one friend here, then. And she had every intention of treasuring her.

* * *

Gabriel took one look at the tableau unfolding before him and wanted to swear long and hard.

One thing the world *didn't* need was another Funaro.

One thing that world *really* didn't need was a Funaro his daughter found irresistible.

Not that he blamed Lili for falling for the statuesque woman who'd folded down to her height with the ease and grace of a ballet dancer. Or who smiled at her as if her very heart's delight had just been handed to her on a diamond-encrusted platinum platter at Lili's announcement.

Even *his* heart had thrilled as he'd watched the scene unfold, and he was a hardened cynic who didn't trust in appearances or believe that anyone in the room had his or Lili's best interests at heart. He watched the stranger rise; watched the way Lili slipped her hand inside her new friend's; noted the way this Audrey's fingers curled around Lili's as if…

He rubbed a hand across his chest.

As if she welcomed that hand. As if she'd keep that little hand safe from all harm. As if…

He swallowed an indigestible lump. It is the way Fina should've held Lili's hand. But even if his wife hadn't died and was still in their midst, that wasn't the kind of woman Fina had been. None of the women in this room were. None of them would hold Lili's hand in that fashion.

He studied the quietly beautiful woman's face with its dark eyes. If one wasn't looking for it, they wouldn't immediately see the beauty there. But he had an artist's eye and recognised it immediately. This wasn't a woman who made the most of her assets by painting her face, by drawing her hair up into a complicated style that took myriad pins and a team of hairdressers to maintain. If her dress and shoes were anything to go by, she wasn't a woman who, before now, had the means to buy designer labels.

Several women in the room exchanged raised eyebrows. As if to say 'Look what the cat has dragged in.'

Mind you, all too soon this Audrey would have access to the funds to rectify every single problem the assorted horde would find with her appearance. And then they'd be jealous of her as she outshone them all.

For a brief moment, at least. Like a star shining its brightest before exploding. Or should that be imploding? Whatever one wanted to call it, it'd be spectacular. And then it'd be spectacularly disastrous.

Marguerite finally made a general introduction to the room at large, saying that she was pleased to welcome her granddaughter Audrey into the family fold. A chair was placed for Audrey beside Marguerite's, and he gave a silent, humourless laugh. Audrey didn't yet understand the honour being done to her with the placement of that chair. But she'd learn. And if she didn't want to be eaten alive by the piranhas in the room, she'd better learn *presto*.

The temperature in the room rose as resentment and *devilry* heated the air. What would most of the people here give to be seated in such close proximity to Marguerite, to have the opportunity to whisper sweet nothings and bitter calumnies in her ear for ten minutes? How many of them would like the opportunity to make a fresh impression on their stately elder?

And because they couldn't, because they'd messed up—in some instances again and again— the feuding family members in the room seemed to momentarily join forces against the newcomer. As if they couldn't wait until she, too, fell from grace.

A bitter sigh welled inside him. He didn't doubt that Audrey would indeed fall from grace. She *was* a Funaro, after all. Falling from grace was what the Funaros did. They knew of no other way of being.

As various family members were called forward to be introduced and pay their respects, he remained in the shadows—where he belonged. He wasn't a member of the family, thank God. He was tolerated as Lili's father, nothing more. Lili might be a Funaro, but she was also a Dimarco. His hands clenched. He would *not* allow her to go the way of her mother. He would *not* allow this family's excesses, their hedonism and extravagances, to destroy his daughter. He would do everything in his power to prevent that from happening.

He kept a close eye on Lili now and it took all his willpower not to call her back to his side. It would bring attention to the both of them, and that was something he'd avoid if he could.

The arrangement—one legally signed off by a team of lawyers—stated that during the summer Lili would spend uninterrupted time with her mother's family. He had no desire to engage in a protracted legal battle with Marguerite if she should happen to take exception to some interference of his, or imagined some slight or infringement to her rights.

Where he could, he'd keep things amicable. To her credit, on this one issue Marguerite had been in surprising agreement. When he'd demanded to be allowed to accompany Lili for her summers at Lake Como, Marguerite had acquiesced. They both knew his being there would keep Lili content and secure. In his turn, he ensured Marguerite could spend time with Lili throughout the rest of the year. They maintained an uneasy peace he would prefer not to shatter.

He glanced again at the newcomer's face and his chest clenched. Her height, the line of her nose and the aristocratic cheekbones pronounced her heritage. He saw Fina there, and her mother, Danae, too.

He would never again fall for a Funaro heiress, never again indulge a fascination for one, or even speak to one longer than necessary. Once had been enough. He would not live that nightmare a second time.

It didn't mean he relished the notion of witnessing another heiress's fall from grace, though. Watching the newcomer succumb to the wealth and sophistication, the petty flatteries and scheming seductions, the endless parties. Breath hissed from his lungs. The drugs.

He loathed the thought of all the potential encased in that elegant frame being brought low; watching as the fire in those eyes dimmed and eventually went out.

'Gabriel!'

His name, an imperial command from the matriarch herself, snapped him back to himself.

'Come! I have a request to make of you.'

He kept his face a study of polite lines. What was the scheming Funaro elder up to now? Whatever it was, he suspected he wouldn't like it.

Lili's wide smile and hopping excitement had him moving towards the trio in the middle of the room, rather than heading for the door like his instincts told him to.

'This is Papa.' Lili leaned against Audrey's legs, smiling up at her with the naive openness and utter assurance of a much-loved four-year-old, clearly believing Audrey adored her every bit as much as Lili did her. It made him want to snatch his daughter up and bolt from the house and lock her in a tower where none of these people could ever hurt her.

'I'm looking forward to meeting your papa,' Audrey said with a wide smile that had a different part of his anatomy jerking to attention. He wrestled with the curse that rose to his lips.

'Good grief, Audrey,' said Marguerite, 'you don't need to stand every time I introduce you to someone new.'

'It only seems polite,' Audrey returned mildly, apparently unfazed by her grandmother's imperial tone.

'Audrey, this is my grandson-in-law. He was married to my granddaughter Serafina.'

'My *mamma*,' Lili whispered. Though four-year-olds apparently couldn't manage a quiet whisper; they only thought they did.

Audrey squeezed Lili's hand. 'And my sister.'

'Half sister,' Marguerite snapped with her customary autocratic tyranny.

Audrey winked at Lili. 'I bet your mamma and I would've been the best of friends.'

A titter went around the room. Quickly quelled by Marguerite's glare. But he silently agreed with everyone else. He doubted Audrey could've made

Fina a friend, but he appreciated the kindness to his daughter.

'Gabriel,' he said, extending his hand as Marguerite had failed to mention that key piece of information.

She promptly placed her hand in his and something arced between them. Something that had her eyes widening and him frowning. They reclaimed their hands at exactly the same moment.

'Audrey apparently has some artistic talent,' Marguerite said peremptorily.

Uh-huh. A dabbler. He lowered his gaze to hide the derision in his eyes, the cynical twist of his mouth.

'She's been studying under Madame De Luca for the last month.'

His head shot up, and the way Audrey's lips twitched made him suspect he'd not hidden his shock very well. If she'd been studying under Madame De Luca, though, she must have a degree of talent.

Audrey registered Gabriel's surprise at the fact she'd been studying under someone so well regarded, and it made her smile.

But that didn't stop her hand from continuing to burn at the brief pressure of his, or help ease the constriction in her chest. This odd awareness didn't make sense. Gabriel wasn't classically handsome. He wasn't smooth or clean-cut or smilingly polished like the other men in the room. What he was, though, was thoroughly masculine. Dark haired, olive skinned and sporting several days' growth of beard, he seemed to *bristle*. Something primitive beat beneath the contained demeanour and it thrilled something primitive deep inside her.

She had no idea what that meant—he probably had that effect on every woman he met. Whatever it was, it was far from comfortable. And she had every intention of ignoring it.

She had enough to negotiate this summer. She wasn't adding men and romance to the mix. She wasn't thinking about any of that until she'd worked out her place in the family; had learned to negotiate this new world of hers.

Grey eyes continued to survey her, their colour taking her off guard. They should be dark like his hair. And yet...

Stop it!

'What medium is your speciality?'

The question had her swallowing. 'While Grandmother is correct, and I have been studying under Madame De Luca, it has been as a favour to a mutual friend of ours. Your first impression was the correct one—I am a rank amateur.'

Expressive brows rose as if he'd noted her evasion. It was just...when she told others her artform of choice, they usually laughed. And she didn't want anyone laughing. Not today. There were already enough undercurrents threading through the room that she didn't understand.

'I'd hate for Grandmother's words to mislead you.'

He stared at her for a long moment, flicked a glance at the rest of the room and nodded. She let out a breath, the tension in her shoulders easing. 'Are you an artist, Gabriel?'

Another titter sounded through the room, and she fought back a frown. What had she said now?

The Funaros might not be as warm as she'd hoped, but it was early days. She hitched up her chin. She'd make them love her yet. Resisting the urge to glance to Marguerite for an explanation, she held Gabriel's gaze and awaited his answer.

'I am a sculptor.' He pushed his hands into his trouser pockets. 'I work with recycled materials.'

'Like?'

'Like steel, wood, wire and such.'

Hold on...

Her heart started to thump. 'Do you work on large installations?'

He nodded.

His first name was Gabriel...

She swallowed. 'You wouldn't happen to be Gabriel Dimarco by any chance, would you?'

'*Si*, that is me.'

Her jaw dropped. She couldn't help it.

'Audrey, please,' Marguerite half sighed, half ordered.

'But—' She stared at her grandmother. 'His work is amazing.' She swung back to him. '*Your* work is amazing.'

Her hands fluttered in the air as if searching for all the things she wanted to say; all the things his work made her feel. She could no more control them than she could the sun—or the rest of the room's opinion of her. But the knowledge she was standing in front of such an artist drove all such concerns momentarily from her mind. Gabriel's installations stood in both public spaces and enviable private collections. He could demand whatever price he wanted. He was a *huge* name in the art world.

'I saw your installation titled *Maybe* in Como. It was the most amazing piece. I sat there for an hour watching how it changed as the sun passed overhead.' It sat in a pretty town square, and the sculpture was an Impressionist piece—half human, half butterfly...or, at least, if not a butterfly, something winged. 'It made me feel hopeful but sad. I couldn't work out if the figure wanted to take flight or return to its cocoon.'

Powerful arms folded across an impressive chest. Considering the tools he must use, he'd need every one of those impressive muscles. 'What was your conclusion?'

She pondered the question anew. 'I spent a lot of time trying to work it out.' She'd gone back the next day, earlier in the morning when the sun would hit it at different angles, to see if that would help her solve the conundrum. 'In the end, I decided it depicted the battle between security and adventure, and that the piece was deliberately ambiguous. I don't think the figure knew yet which it was going to choose.'

Grey eyes widened and nostrils flared. 'You—'

He snapped back whatever he'd been about to say with a shake of his head. 'I am glad you enjoyed the piece.'

She wanted to press him for what he'd been going to say, but it wouldn't be polite. And she suspected her grandmother would find it indecorous. Twice already this afternoon Marguerite had heaved a sigh and murmured, 'Dear Lord, Audrey, we're really going to have to take you in hand.'

She had no idea what that meant. She hoped it wasn't as ominous as it sounded. She liked Marguerite, and an additional point in the older woman's favour was the fact she clearly loved her great-granddaughter. She and Lili seemed to have a perfect understanding.

She was far from sure about the rest of the room, however. She'd seen the raised eyebrows, the speaking glances. She suspected she'd been meant to. Why didn't they want to embrace her the way she wanted to embrace them?

Was it about the money?

Surely not. The Funaro family had so much wealth that one more person sharing a portion of it wouldn't make any difference. Not that she wanted a portion of it. She just wanted the family. And she was determined to find a way to bring them around.

'What I would like for you to do, Gabriel,' Marguerite said now, 'is take Audrey's art education in hand. Determine where she's at and what she needs—' that imperious hand waved through the air '—and then use your connections to engage whatever teachers, tutors or experts you deem necessary.'

Audrey blinked. 'Grandmother, that's something you ought to consult with me about first.'

The room froze. Very slowly, Marguerite turned her head to meet Audrey's gaze, and the expression in her eyes had her gulping. 'It's just…' It took a superhuman effort to not wince, grimace, or backtrack. 'It'll be expensive to hire experts like that, and I've already told you I'm not here for your money. The money might not mean a lot to you, but…' It meant a lot to her and she didn't want anyone here thinking she was only out for what she could get.

Her grandmother gestured for Audrey to bend down. Hiding a wince, she did as she bid and prayed the older woman wasn't going to yell at high volume in her ear.

'Please…'

The word was nothing more than a whisper, but she heard the vulnerability threaded through it and it had tears prickling the backs of her eyes. Straightening, she swallowed and eventually nodded, turning back to Gabriel. 'I would be very grateful for any advice you'd be able to offer. If you have the time.'

When she was sure nobody was looking, she reached down and squeezed her grandmother's hand. 'Thank you.'

'Papa, can Audrey come with us to your studio tomorrow?'

'I think that's a remarkably fine idea, Lili.' A gleam lit Marguerite's eyes. 'Do you have any objections, Gabriel?'

The pulse in his jaw ticked. 'None whatsoever,' he eventually ground out.

Audrey's heart plummeted. Oh, God. He didn't want her invading his studio space. How on earth could she get out of this gracefully and save face for everyone?

'Be ready to leave at nine o'clock.'

'She'll be ready,' Marguerite said.

Before she could think of a way to extricate herself, Gabriel was already striding away. She glanced down at her grandmother, recalled her *please* and swallowed her protests, made herself smile. 'What a treat! Thank you.'

CHAPTER TWO

THE FOLLOWING MORNING Audrey made sure to be sitting on one of the hard-backed chairs in the foyer ten minutes before the assigned time. She had no intention of being late or putting anyone out more than they already had been.

Recalling again the less than thrilled expression on Gabriel's face, she grimaced. She didn't blame him for his lack of enthusiasm. He was an important artist. He was probably working on something amazing. He didn't need the likes of her underfoot.

Biting at a hangnail on her thumb, she made a resolution to do her best to remain in the background and not get in the way.

After pulling the thumb from her mouth, she clasped both hands in her lap. Apparently, Funaros didn't fidget. Apparently, they were always careful to appear composed and at ease, regardless of how they felt inside. The thing was she also happened to be a Martinelli, and they *did* fidget, and they had a habit of wearing their hearts on their sleeves.

She glanced up when the front door swung open to see Lili come skipping through it, her father following close behind. *Not* skipping. She shot to her feet and the little girl threw her arms around Audrey's legs, the little face smiling up at her with big shining eyes. Audrey swept her up in her arms and hugged her back. She had a niece! It made her want to dance.

Before any of them could speak, a door off to the left opened and Marguerite strode out. At seventy-four she was still as erect as she must've been as a much younger woman. Audrey envied her poise. She doubted she'd ever acquire that level of grace and command, no matter how hard she practised.

'Good morning, Audrey and Liliana. Gabriel.'

Clearly, Marguerite wasn't the kind of person to enjoy a morning lie-in.

Audrey set Lili back on her feet. 'Good morning, Grandmother.'

'Marguerite.' Gabriel nodded in the older woman's direction. 'Gently!' he ordered Lili as she raced across to hug her great-grandmother in the same way she had Audrey.

'Leave the child be, Gabriel. I'm not as frail as you and the rest of the family make me out to be.'

Marguerite clearly adored Lili, and while she might try to hide it beneath a crusty exterior, Audrey doubted she was fooling anyone. Least of all, Lili's father. She turned to Gabriel with a grin, expecting him to be amused, too, but he didn't so much as smile. The flat expression in his eyes as he stared back at her had the smile sliding off her lips. Pressing her hands to her waist, she reminded them to neither twist nor fidget.

'Now, Lili, I have a proposition for you. Tomaso

informs me it's time to decide which puppy we're to keep from Tippy's litter.'

Lili's eyes grew wide. 'Can we play with them yet?'

'We can.'

The little girl hopped from one foot to the other. 'When?'

'This morning, and as it's the only morning I have free this week, I'm afraid you'll need to decide if you want to accompany your father and Audrey to the studio, or if you'd like to come to the stables and play with the puppies and help me choose which one to keep.'

Lili swung to her father. 'Can I stay with Nonna, Papa? *Please?* I want to play with the puppies.'

His jaw tightened fractionally and Audrey wondered if Marguerite noticed it, too. 'Do you mean to abandon your new friend so quickly, Lili?'

That little face fell and Audrey found herself crouching down in front of her. 'I totally understand, Lili. I mean…puppies, right?'

The little girl's relief was palpable and then her entire face lit up. 'We could *all* stay and play with the puppies!'

'No.'

The single word shot from Gabriel's mouth like a bullet and they all jumped.

'I mean,' he moderated his voice, no doubt for his daughter's benefit, 'that I shall be going to the studio today as planned. Audrey will have to make the decision whether to stay and play with the puppies or come to the studio for herself.'

Puppies would win in the ordinary course of events. And the 'No Trespassing' signals radiating from Gabriel in waves would normally seal the deal. But her grandmother drew herself up to her full height and sent her a look that told Audrey in no uncertain terms what was expected of her. Yet, it was that vulnerable *please* from last night that played through her mind.

'I've no desire to change our plans. I'm looking forward to seeing your studio.'

His lips twisted and his jaw clenched as if he was biting back something curt and succinct. His nose didn't exactly curl, but it felt like it did and she could feel herself shrivelling inside.

A Funaro always appears composed.

She planted as pleasant a smile as she could to her face and kept her chin high. She'd get this done—go and tour his studio, have a brief conversation about her artistic endeavours—to please Marguerite. She'd get the names of several suitable teachers whom she could contact, and then she and Gabriel need never have anything to do with each other again.

'Liliana, pop through the kitchen to Maria. I believe she has something special for you.'

With a wave, Lili raced off in the direction of the kitchen.

'A word if you don't mind, Gabriel. We won't be a minute, Audrey.'

Another flaring of those rather savage nostrils had Audrey internally quailing, but when Marguerite turned on her very elegant heel and strode back the way she'd come, he fell into step behind her.

Audrey took a seat and waited. It was no hardship. The villa was utterly extraordinary, and the foyer was all classic white marble with a vaulted ceiling housing a stunning chandelier whose crystals glittered in the light pouring in at the arched windows set high above. And complementing it all was the sweeping curve of a grand staircase.

'I am Cinderella.' She pinched herself. Rather than a fairy godmother, she had a grandmother.

And a niece!

She didn't have long to luxuriate in all the splendour, though. Less than five minutes later Gabriel appeared—turbulent, dark and crackling with barely restrained...um, energy. Without a glance in her direction, he strode out the door.

Was she supposed to follow him? For one brief moment she considered chickening out.

Please.

Marguerite's simple request with its underlying vulnerability pierced through her cowardice. Swearing under her breath, she leapt up and scrambled after him, catching him up before he reached the car.

He didn't utter a word, just slid inside the dark sedan. She moved to the passenger side but when she tried the door handle, it was locked. She had to tap on the window to get him to open it. For one awfully fraught moment she thought he wouldn't; thought he'd drive away and leave her there.

For heaven's sake! There was reasonable annoyance, but then there was also unreasonable rudeness.

He unlocked the door. She slid into her seat, pulled her seatbelt on and folded her hands in her lap.

Don't make waves. Don't rock the boat. Wait until you know how everything here fits together.

It took a superhuman effort, but she bit her tongue and kept her thoughts to herself. She didn't like confrontation. Nobody did, she supposed, but something about this man and his behaviour had her itching to take him to task.

She risked a glance at his profile as he set the car in motion and had to stifle a laugh. Take him to task? He looked like granite—hard and inflexible. She doubted anything she said or did would have the slightest effect on him.

He didn't speak, so she kept her gaze trained directly out to the front.

Comfortable? No. But luckily, the trip took less than ten minutes.

She blinked when he pulled the car to a halt in the carpark of a small marina. If she turned her head, she could see the Funaro Villa back along the lake, its grand arched balconies shining white in the morning sun.

He pushed out of the car so she did, too. Clearing her throat, she prayed her voice would sound normal. 'Where's the studio?'

He pointed at the water, before striding down to the dock towards a speedboat.

Her jaw dropped. An island? His studio was on an island?

And then she couldn't help it; she started to laugh.

'What's so funny?' he said with an irritable twist of his lips, though he did have the civility to help her step into the boat.

Where was she supposed to sit? He didn't give her any hints, so she chose the padded seat beside the driver's seat. It might not be large, but the boat looked built for speed, and this seat had handrails to the front and side for her to hold on to. Did he have any lifejackets?

'Under the seat,' he said, as if reading her mind.

She put it on. To her surprise he put one on, too.

'Can you swim?'

She nodded. 'Can you?'

He nodded back. *That* was the extent of their conversation before he fired up the engine, undid the moorings and turned the boat's nose towards the middle of the lake.

They'd been travelling for five minutes, maybe a bit longer, when he cut the engine and she turned from admiring the view. Lake Como, the lakeside villas dotted here and there, the forests and mountains... Dear God, it was *breathtaking*.

'You didn't tell me why you laughed back there on shore.'

'I didn't,' she agreed, determined to keep a pleas-

ant expression on her face. It would be good practise. If she could maintain her equilibrium around
this man, she suspected the rest of mankind would
be a walk in the park.

'You do not wish to tell me?'

Be pleasant.

'It's just…the way you people live. It's extraordinary, and so far removed from my usual world
it boggles my mind.'

Dark eyebrows rose. '*You* people?'

'The Funaros and—'

'I am *not* a Funaro!'

Wow, okay. 'But you're clearly from the same
world and—'

'I did not grow up with the kind of wealth and
privilege that the members of the Funaro family
were fortunate enough to enjoy.' Stern lips became
positively grim. 'I am not of the same social standing or—'

He broke off, breathing hard. She'd clearly struck
a nerve.

Keep your equilibrium, Cinders.

'Well, let's stick to the facts, then,' she said
pleasantly. She held up one finger. 'You're ridiculously successful and wealthy.' She held up another. 'You have an art studio on an island in the
middle of Lake Como.' She held up a third finger.
'And you're famous. This is not the usual state of
affairs for the majority of people.'

Hooded eyes surveyed her for a moment. 'The

studio is not on an island. It's simply located farther around the lake.'

'Oh, well, then that makes everything *ordinary*, then.'

Her eyeroll and the loud breath that shot from her lungs ruined the pleasant thing she'd had going. She comforted herself with the thought that she was a work in progress and that the poise would come with time.

'Signor Dimarco—'

'Gabriel!' he growled, a scowl darkening his face.

In that moment she decided pleasantness was highly overrated. With a superhuman effort, she didn't growl back. She folded her hands in her lap and met his gaze. 'Do you have friends?'

He blinked as if the question was the last thing he'd expected. 'Of course, I do. I have many in Milan where I live. Not so many here around Lake Como, that is true. Why?'

'Are they nice, good, decent people?'

Grey eyes narrowed. 'I think so. Why?'

'It's just that I'm interested in how you manage to keep them if this is the way you treat people.'

His hands clenched so hard he started to shake. Reaching down, she trailed her finger through the water. 'At least the water temperature is pleasant.'

'For what?'

'For if you really do plan to throw me overboard.'

The thunderous expression that raced across his face had her eyes widening, and no amount of coaching herself to remain composed could prevent it. But a moment later she was released from the fierce glare when he ran a hand over his face.

With a soft curse he eventually met her gaze once more, his expression milder. Or at least what she suspected he hoped would appear milder. It was debatable if *mild* was something this man could achieve. 'This is something you fear from me?'

Not really, but… 'I don't know you. I've been thrust upon you in a way that you obviously resent, and yet for some reason you didn't refuse when Marguerite made her request yesterday. You don't want me here. You've made that very clear. You've barely been civil. One could even say you've been actively rude.'

He blinked. 'I—'

'I'm sorry I couldn't find an excuse to get out of the studio visit in a way that would've seemed polite to my grandmother. But you have my assurance that I will do my best to stay out of your way when we reach your studio, and to take up as little of your time as possible.'

Grey eyes throbbed into hers.

She swallowed when he didn't say anything. 'And then, when we return to the villa, we need barely see each other again.'

'That will be impossible.'

She stared down at her hands and huffed out a laugh. 'Oh, I'm sure you'll find a way.'

'Lili.' He said his daughter's name as if it explained all. 'Unless I'm very much mistaken, you are as taken with my daughter as she is with you.'

Damn.

'She will wish to spend time with you.'

She wanted to spend time with Lili, too. She studied his face, blew out a breath. 'And you don't allow your daughter to spend time with people you don't know.'

'I do not,' he agreed.

She couldn't blame him for that.

'I owe you an apology, Audrey. I did not mean to take my bad temper out on you. You are right. I have treated you abominably and I humbly ask your forgiveness.'

It was her turn to blink. She, um…wow, okay. 'Consider it forgotten,' she mumbled.

They stared at each other. She couldn't read the expression in his eyes at all. 'What does your grandmother have on you?' he finally asked.

She wasn't sure she'd heard him correctly. 'I beg your pardon?'

'Why do you feel compelled to do Marguerite's bidding? What does she blackmail you with?'

'She's not blackmailing me!'

She leaned towards him, but it brought her in too close. His scent hit her and it was like a shock of cold water to her senses. She shot back, her heart pounding.

Stop being ridiculous.

And yet a strange new energy filled her, and it took all her strength to not lean forward and breathe him in a second time. Something about him invigorated her like a cold alpine breeze and sea spray, but it carried the heat of chilli peppers. That heat stole into her veins now.

She did what she could to shake the sensation off. 'Marguerite has unreservedly welcomed me into her family and her home. She's been kind and generous and everything that is benevolent. In asking you to assist me with my art, she's hoping to provide me with something that will make me happy. It would be ungrateful, not to mention ungracious, for me to refuse her that.'

He remained unmoved.

She started to lean towards him again, but caught herself in time. 'We're family, Gabriel. Family should pull together and look after one another. I know it's only early days, but that's what I would like to work towards with Marguerite.' It's what she'd like to work towards with all of the family.

'Then you are a fool.'

She turned and stared at the water, doing her best to rein in her temper. When she was pretty certain she'd managed it, she turned back. 'I thought you weren't going to be rude anymore.'

'I did not mean to be rude. I am simply telling you the truth. If you think Marguerite has your best interests at heart, then you are sadly mistaken.'

He loathed the Funaro family. Folding her arms, she swallowed. 'What's your reading of the situation, then?'

'Marguerite's only concern is to maintain the prestige of the Funaro name, nothing more.'

She recalled that *please*, the expression in her grandmother's eyes when they rested on Lili. 'I think you're mistaken.'

'And what if I were to tell you she is already regretting the rather spontaneous request she made of me?'

Her mouth went strangely dry. 'For what reason?'

'Because it belatedly occurred to her that I might taint another of her precious granddaughters.'

Her heart pounded against the walls of her ribs. 'That's what her *quick word* was about?'

Stern lips cracked open in a humourless smile. 'It was indeed.'

Her grandmother had *warned him off*? She didn't know whether to be offended or absurdly touched.

'Succeed in resisting my masculine charms, Audrey, and the plaudits will be yours.'

He stretched out his arms as if he were a prize or a trophy. She swallowed and shifted on her seat. The thing was she couldn't deny that he had a lot of masculine charm. Not that it meant anything. She wasn't going to pursue him or anything.

'Fail and allow yourself to be seduced by me, and you'll be considered a bitter disappointment and relegated to the ranks and ignored like everyone else.'

He didn't want to seduce her, that much was clear, and yet his words and their accompanying smile sent a chill racing down her spine. Along with a traitorous and wholly unwelcome thrill.

CHAPTER THREE

UNABLE TO STARE AT the incredulous expression on Audrey's far too expressive face a moment longer, Gabriel kicked the boat's engine back over with a curse and turned in the direction of his studio. He was careful, though, to keep the action of the boat as smooth as he could as an unfamiliar shame washed through him.

All of the anger and resentment he'd wanted to fling at Marguerite, all of the bitterness he felt towards Fina and the Funaro name, he'd just taken out on Audrey. Marguerite had disturbed old ghosts, but Audrey didn't deserve to bear his anger for that.

It took all his willpower not to lower his head to the steering wheel and give in to the exhaustion that crashed down on him. He and Lili had been at the Funaro estate for two weeks, and already he felt stretched to his limit. He had another ten weeks of this *imprisonment* to go. How would he bear it?

Gritting his teeth, he shoved his shoulders back. He would bear whatever was necessary for Lili's sake. He understood Marguerite's game—she hoped that if she made him uncomfortable enough, he would leave Lili with her for the duration of the summer and return to Milan.

His hands tightened on the wheel. *That* wasn't going to happen.

Blowing out a breath, he glanced at the woman beside him. Dismissing her as just another Funaro was far from fair. The stunned expression on her face just now... He shook his head. This woman was completely unaware of her position as a pawn on the Funaro chessboard.

She was still an innocent. One who believed in the sanctity of family. One who took what people told her at face value. One who clearly believed the best of people rather than the worst.

His lips twisted. Over the course of the summer, as she discovered the *delights* of the Funaro lifestyle, he had no doubts that she, too, would change and adopt their ways, become lost to the glamour, the partying... The jockeying for position and Marguerite's favour. She'd become hard and sophisticated, devious and disingenuous, shrewd and conniving. Unscrupulous.

Maybe not, a tiny voice whispered. Maybe she'd walk away when she discovered what they were.

Family should pull together and look after one another.

Or they would break her and she would flee back home.

Which he suddenly realised he had no knowledge of, beyond the fact it was Australia.

Very gently, he brought the boat in beside the studio's tiny dock, slipped a rope over the mooring post and secured it fast. After leaping out, he held a hand out towards Audrey, but she remained seated. 'Can I say something before we do this?' She nodded at the path that led to the studio.

'Of course.'

That pointed chin lifted. 'I make my own decisions about who I date and when I date.'

Dark eyes flashed, and although he stood on firm ground, he had to widen his stance to keep his balance.

'Let me make this very clear. I'm not currently in the market for either a boyfriend or a lover.'

The way her lips shaped the word *lover* had heat licking along his veins. He had to ignore it. He had no intention—*none whatsoever*—of dallying with this woman.

'And you can act as cynical and mocking as you like, but I'm fully aware that a man like you wouldn't be interested in someone like me.'

What on earth…?

'So if you *are* plotting to seduce me with a view to aggravating Marguerite, you can forget about it.'

He wasn't planning any such thing!

'I'm not going to fall for it. And you can rest assured I won't be instigating any kind of flirtation with you either, so you can stop already with the exaggerated sighs and black looks.'

With the *what*?

'I'm fully aware that I'm neither polished nor beautiful, but nor am I an idiot and—'

'Your beauty is undeniable.' Maybe he shouldn't

have said it, but he couldn't allow it to go unchallenged.

She blinked.

'It's true you're not polished, but look at the land behind me.' He gestured at the unmanicured woodland that surrounded his studio and cut it off from the rest of civilisation. 'It is not polished either, but one cannot deny its beauty. One can acquire polish if they wish to.'

She stared at him as if she didn't know what to say.

'In fact, Marguerite will require it of you.'

Something in her eyes dimmed, but a moment later she shook herself, and her expression became resolute once again. 'I just wanted us on the same page about…all of that. So you've no need to be so…'

He crouched down so that they were eye to eye, and her scent rose up around him. It was wholesome and restful…familiar. It took him a moment to place it. *Lavender.* She smelled of lavender. It made him want to smile. 'No need to be so…?'

'Guarded, I suppose. Suspicious. Disapproving. You don't know me and yet I feel you've already condemned me.'

He bit back a sigh. 'If I have been sighing and glaring, it's not because of you.'

One eyebrow rose. 'I'm not sure I believe you.'

Her words were like knives and he didn't know

why they should sting him so. 'I am not a dishonest man. I do not lie.'

Eyes the colour of cloves scanned his face now, but he couldn't tell if she believed him or not. 'Then what has the sighing and glaring been about?'

'Marguerite.'

Both brows shot up. 'You're still brooding about that?'

'She is manipulative and imperious. I do not like to be manipulated.' His lips twisted. 'Or given orders.'

He rose and held out his hand. 'Will you now disembark?'

She took his hand, her fingers tightening in his as the boat rocked. But she didn't panic, merely looked for him to tell her where to put her feet, and before he was ready, she was standing in front of him, swamping him in the comforting scent of lavender.

He went to release her, but her hand tightened in his. 'Please tell me you believe I've no designs on you.'

'Of course, I believe you.' And he did. 'I have been rude and boorish and you have felt threatened by me—for which I again apologise. I cannot imagine you would wish to lumber yourself with such a bad-tempered lover. No sensible woman would. And I believe that you are very sensible.'

Her lips twitched. It told him she no longer felt

threatened by him, and he gave thanks for it. The thought of frightening any woman, let alone one as alone as Audrey, made him sick to his stomach.

'Also, you spoke of beauty earlier as if it were a precursor to embarking upon an affair,' he continued, 'and I cannot be accused of being a beautiful man.'

'No,' she agreed, finally releasing him. 'But there is something compelling about you.'

A pulse inside him burst to life. He ignored it. Refused to allow himself to consider her words too closely.

She cocked her head to one side. 'Beauty and attraction don't necessarily go hand in hand.'

Dio! Was she saying—?

She stiffened as if suddenly realising how her words could be interpreted. Coughing, she hastened back into speech. 'Besides, a person is so much more than what they look like. There's a woman I work with back home.'

Did she not now consider *this* her home?

'When you first meet her, you might think her plain, but when you get to know her, you realise she's one of the most beautiful people you'll ever meet.'

Affection brightened her eyes, and her lips curved in a way that had him catching his breath. When Audrey let her guard down, she—

She nothing!

He gestured for her to precede him on the path. 'Where do you work?'

'At a nursing home in Melbourne—an aged care facility.'

'You are a nurse?'

'More a nurse's aide, really. I didn't study nursing at university or anything.'

'Why not?'

She was quiet for a moment, before sending him a swift smile. 'I was busy with other things.'

He sensed she didn't wish to discuss it, and let the matter drop. After having been so ill-tempered, he needed to prove he could be a pleasant host now. Climbing the short rise in the path and then rounding the curve, his studio came into view and Audrey came to a dead halt. He only just managed to avoid walking into her.

Clasping her hands together, she stared at it with wide eyes. 'Oh, Gabriel, I think you are the luckiest man alive.'

'This is my summer sanctuary. Here I can retreat from the pressures of the Funaro family and lose myself in my art.'

At least, that had been the plan—it is what had happened in previous summers—but his art wasn't providing him with the respite, comfort or distraction it usually did. Instead, in failing him, it had become another source of tension.

He pushed that thought away. 'It is where Lili and I can come for some quiet time—to picnic and swim if we so desire.' And to sleep, too, on occasion. There were sleeping quarters here. The Funaros didn't own this land. It was his and his alone. Here Marguerite had no sovereignty, and he was determined to keep it that way.

She swung around, her face falling. 'And I'm intruding. *That's* why you've been in such a bad mood.'

He wrinkled his nose. 'I…'

'You told me you don't lie.' Her hands went to her hips. 'Don't disappoint me now.'

He stared at his studio, letting out a long breath. 'I have never invited any member of the family to my studio before. I do not wish for their dramas and demands to sully this place.'

'And you haven't invited me now, either.' With a wistful glance in the studio's direction, she turned back to him and squared her shoulders. 'Marguerite has been unreasonable, Gabriel. Come,' she said, gesturing for him to turn around. 'Return me to the villa. I'm sorry you've been put to so much trouble. I'll explain to Marguerite that she had no right to ask this of you. You can keep your sanctuary safe and—'

'I would be honoured to share it with you.'

He wasn't sure who was more surprised by his offer, him or Audrey.

'You are an artist, are you not?' he demanded, not allowing himself to dwell on why he was willing to share this special place with her.

She huffed out a laugh. 'That's debatable.'

'When you get the opportunity, do you lose yourself in your work for as long as you can? When you are working on something, do you think about it all the time? When you cannot make the vision in your head a reality and everything you do fails, and the frustration builds and builds until you think you will burst, do you keep persisting because you cannot let it go? And when you have a breakthrough, can see a way forward, does it feel like you are flying?'

Her jaw dropped. Nodding, she dragged it back into place. Satisfaction rippled through him. An artist created, and Audrey clearly created. It didn't matter if others saw value in her work or not. It didn't matter if *he* saw value in her work or not. In that moment, though, he burned with a strange curiosity to see what it was that she made.

'Would you continue with your art whether people said it was good, bad or indifferent?'

'Yes.' The word was quietly uttered, but strong for all that.

'Then, Audrey, you are an artist. It is what you do.' He gestured towards his studio. 'Would you like to see inside?'

'Very much.'

'Then come.'

Without another word, he led her to the studio door and unlocked it. 'Ready?'

'For what?' she asked, entering behind.

He flicked a switch on the wall and her eyes widened as the steel shutters on the wall of glass directly in front of them slid up to reveal the re-markable view outside. Her mouth formed a per-fect O and he couldn't help but smile. She swung to him, stared at him, then turned back to the view. 'Did I mention earlier that you are the lucki-est man alive?'

He laughed. Here in this space it was easy to laugh, to relax, to be himself. 'I believe you did.'

'You get to work here whenever you want.'

'Not quite. I have a warehouse studio in Milan, which is where I work on my larger pieces. It would not be practical to work on them here. But yes, this is where I work in the summer—on smaller pieces, on sketches and ideas for bigger projects.'

'Oh, Gabriel, it's absolutely amazing. Show me around.'

He gave her a tour, showing her where he kept his materials and the tools of his trade, along with the various projects he was working on. His lips twisted—*trying* to work on, he amended silently.

In her turn, she asked intelligent questions—where did he source his materials? What did he do with the scrap? How long did he spend sketch-ing before starting a sculpture? She gazed at it all, and behind the warm, spice-brown of her eyes he sensed her mind racing.

'It's absolutely amazing—all of it. The light and the view…the tranquillity.'

The quality of the light was why he'd bought the land. Ensuring he made the most of that light had driven the specifications for the building. He'd paid a fortune for it all, but as far as he was concerned it was worth every penny. The tranquillity, though, had sealed the deal. This view looked southward. From here, one couldn't see the Funaro Villa. Nothing here rang a false note or had painful memories clamouring to the surface. All was simple and breathtaking beauty.

She pointed. 'You have a mezzanine level?'

'There are sleeping quarters up there.' He had no intention of giving her a tour of those.

She smiled. 'For when you get too caught up in your work and can't bear to leave.'

For when he needed a break from the Funaros.

'It's all very impressive. Mostly, though, I'm in awe of your work.' She gestured to the nearby bench and the finished work he'd brought with him from Milan that he'd been hoping would inspire him—an Impressionist sculpture of an oak tree in the autumn when its leaves had started to fall. 'I could look at this all day. It's a bit dishevelled and shabby but so strong, so…timeless.' She turned to him. 'You have an amazing talent.'

'Thank you.'

He had been given this compliment before, but her simple sincerity touched him in a way few previous compliments had. 'Now it is your turn to share something of your work with me.'

Her throat bobbed convulsively, and she gripped her hands so hard the knuckles turned white. 'But...' She swallowed again. 'I didn't bring any of it with me.'

He gestured to the small backpack she carried. 'You must have pictures on your phone.' He understood an artist's reluctance to share their work, their concern that it would not be understood... The fear of criticism. It was also important for an artist to overcome such fears. One could learn much from constructive criticism.

'You do not trust me with your art?' The thought pierced him.

'You're an important artist. I am a nobody.'

His brows rose. She was a *Funaro*.

'Very few people consider what I do as art.'

'This was also the fate of Vincent Van Gogh— he was considered unsuccessful and a failure. You are in good company.'

Her nose wrinkled. 'I don't have those kinds of pretensions.'

He was silent for a long moment and then gestured around. 'I have shared all of this with you willingly. Will you not share a little of your art with me?'

'You make me sound churlish.'

She nibbled on her bottom lip and he tried not

to notice the way it deepened the colour; the way that lip grew plump and inviting.

Her shoulders suddenly slumped. 'You promise you won't laugh?'

Who had laughed at her art? 'I promise.'

After pulling her phone from her bag, she opened a photo folder. Clutching it to her chest she met his gaze, grimaced. 'While you look at these, would it be okay if I were to go and explore out there?' She pointed beyond the window.

'Of course.' She didn't want to watch his face as he assessed her work. He had a good poker face, but this woman was proving surprisingly perceptive. 'The door is in the side wall there.'

Without a word, she disappeared through it.

He opened the folder on her phone.

CHAPTER FOUR

AUDREY DIDN'T PACE the path outside that extraordinary wall of glass. She ached to give vent to the nerves stabbing through her, but Gabriel would see. And she didn't want to betray herself like that.

She couldn't work him out. He'd been so rude earlier, and then shocked when she'd called him out on it. As if he'd been so deep inside his own tangled thoughts, he hadn't realised how he'd come across.

Since then, though, he'd been the perfect host.

To stop from turning and staring at him through the wall of glass, and possibly surprising him in the act of curling his lip as he flicked through her so-called *artworks*, she made her way down to the waterfront and a pretty, protected curve of bay. This must be where he and Lili sometimes swam. Kicking off her shoes, she welcomed the cool of the water against her toes.

The water was clear—unruffled and satin soft, the pebbles and sand at her feet easy to negotiate— and the forest around the lake shaded a deep healthy green, while the ridges that rose up all around were harmoniously majestic. Across the lake the buildings of a town glowed cream, yellow and warm ochre in the late-morning sun. Tiny waves splashed against the shore, and the scent of gardenias drifted on the air.

But none of it soothed the agitation rolling through her. The elevated heart rate, the alternate hot and cold flushes. She glanced at her watch and wrung her hands. He'd been looking at the photos on her phone for fifteen minutes! *Oh, God.* She hid her face in her hands. She couldn't believe the celebrated Gabriel Dimarco was currently assessing *her* work.

I don't lie.

Well, maybe he could make an exception this one time, and tell her he thought the pieces pretty and decorative and recommend a teacher or two. Then they could change the subject and never speak of it again.

'What are you afraid you're going to hear?'

She spun to find Gabriel standing on the path above her. Her heart practically hammered its way out of her chest.

'What do you think I'm going to say?'

I don't lie.

Well then, she wouldn't, either. 'That you think the work is trivial and of no consequence.' She kept her chin high. 'Saying that, though, makes it sound as if I have delusions of grandeur when I don't.'

In two steps he was at her side though she couldn't work out how he'd moved so quickly. 'Others have belittled your work?'

'You've seen my medium.' For God's sake, what she did was glorified embroidery—*needlework*. She didn't create post-Impressionist watercolours or grand oil paintings or extraordinary sculptures. She *sewed*. 'I mean, anyone with half a brain can learn to sew, right?'

'Just as anyone with half a brain can slap paint on a canvas or make something from clay. But just because they can, doesn't mean they're good at it.'

His vehemence made her blink.

'But these—' he held up her phone '—are extraordinary, Audrey.'

Had he just said...? Folding her arms to hide the way her hands suddenly shook, she drew herself up to her full height. At five foot ten inches in her bare feet, her full height was pretty impressive, but she still had to throw her head back to meet Gabriel's gaze. 'Don't lie to me. Not about this.'

'I don't lie. This I have already told you.' He waved an impatient hand through the air. 'It is true that when Marguerite asked me to look over your work, I didn't have high hopes. At best I thought you would be a competent amateur. Until she mentioned Madame De Luca.'

'Like I said, that was just a favour for a friend.'

'She does not do such things. Her standards are too high.' Those grey eyes surveyed her with an unblinking certainty that had her pulse easing. 'She might have told you that, let you believe it for whatever reason...probably to keep you humble, but where art is concerned, Madame De Luca does not lower her standards.'

Had Aunt Beatrice deliberately let her believe it

was an arrangement between friends? But why...?
Oh, Lord! Had Beatrice paid the outrageous fees
Madame charged and didn't want Audrey find-
ing out, so had concocted the fiction? Oh! But—

Gabriel shook the phone in front of her face, re-
capturing her attention. 'I'm telling you that you
have a rare talent. Your work is powerful. And
while it is also true that it is sometimes raw, none
of it is insipid. It is infused with life and...'

She leaned towards him, hanging on his every
word. His scent once again an electrifying jolt to
her senses, but this time she welcomed the oddly
enlivening sting of it.

'Emotion.'

Her throat went oddly tight and she had to press
a hand to her breastbone to stop her heart from
falling at her feet.

'Which comes first—the subject or the emotion?'

She'd never pondered that before. 'Sometimes
it's the emotion, but more often it's the subject,'
she said slowly. 'But when I'm working, even if
I don't want it to, the emotion takes over and di-
rects everything.'

He nodded.

She held herself on such a tight leash in her everyday life, always had—had needed to—and art
had become her outlet.

'Did not Madame De Luca tell you of your talent?'

'She told me I had an excellent technique and

that my work showed promise. But I thought she was just being kind.'

He raised his eyes heavenward, exclaiming, *'Dio!'* before grey eyes skewered her to the spot once again. 'Did your family, your Australian family, belittle your work? Is that why you have feared my assessment? If I'd known how concerned you were I wouldn't have left you hanging so long.'

'No! I mean, I don't think they really understood it, none of them are artistic, but Nonna and my cousin Frankie have always been ridiculously amazed and encouraging.' So had Johanna.

'Rightly amazed,' he corrected. 'Your father?'

She shrugged, her chest clenching at the mention of her father. 'He's more the mad scientist type. If it's not part of the imperial table of elements or has a formula an arm long, he doesn't recognise it.'

'I cannot believe you have gone undiscovered for so long.'

It was no surprise to her. 'I've never attended an art class or studied art at university. I just…dabble in my spare time. There's absolutely no reason why I should've been discovered.' She frowned. 'And you might change your mind once you see my pieces in the flesh.'

She wished she hadn't used the phrase *in the flesh*. Uttering those words at Gabriel seemed altogether too suggestive.

Something in his eyes flared, but it was quickly extinguished. 'I do not think so.'

She couldn't get her head around this conversation at all. He truly thought she had talent?

'I know of several teachers who would help you hone your craft.'

He did?

'Alas, they are all in Rome and Florence, though I think that I, too, could help.'

She moistened suddenly dry lips. 'You would consider taking me on as a student?' He was famously reclusive when it came to discussing his work. Rumour had it that many young artists had petitioned him for a mentorship, but all had been refused. Would he seriously make an exception for her?

'Our mediums are different, but many of our goals are the same.' Firm lips twisted. 'And as we're both stuck here for the summer... Think it over and—'

'I don't need to think about it. I would love to learn all I could from you, Gabriel. I'm fully aware of the compliment you pay me.'

'Good.' He nodded. 'I request, however, that you do not speak to the newspapers about this. I value my privacy.'

'You have my word.'

He stared at her for a long moment, and the air between them crackled. 'You have something else to say?' he demanded.

She chewed on the inside of her lip. 'Are you sure about this?'

His chin tilted at an unconsciously arrogant angle. 'I am not in the habit of making offers that I am not sure about. Why?'

She swallowed. 'Marguerite hasn't asked this of you, has she?' The thought of being foisted on him had everything inside her protesting.

'No. If she had I would not have made the offer.' A humourless smile touched his lips. 'In fact, she will probably be vexed by the arrangement.'

Which, as far as he was concerned, was a point in its favour, she realised.

Those grey eyes turned mocking. 'Do you dare risk her displeasure, Audrey? Which comes first—family or art?'

'Family.' She didn't even have to think about it.

He blinked.

'But I expect Marguerite will be fully cognizant of the honour you do me in offering to mentor me.' She nodded slowly, recalling the vulnerability in her grandmother's eyes. *Please.* 'I suspect she would consider me a fool if I were to refuse it.'

She *would* be a fool. This was a once-in-a-lifetime opportunity. Knowing her own weaknesses, though, knowing how much she yearned for family, if she wasn't careful the Funaro family would consume her completely. And that would defeat the purpose of being here. Accepting Gabriel's offer could help her prevent that from happening.

She wanted to be considered a legitimate member of the Funaro family, but she didn't want to lose her own identity. Or turn her back on her past. A chill chased down her spine. Accepting Gabriel's offer, having a chance to focus on her art, would give her something that was just her own, and might help her find a way to bridge past and present.

'Before we embark any further on this discussion, I need to make one thing very clear to you, Audrey.' His voice had gone chillingly serious and she met his gaze once more. 'I will not shackle myself to the Funaro family a second time.'

For a moment she didn't know what he was talking about. Then she stiffened. 'Didn't we just talk about this?'

'Is that clear?' he repeated, his brows drawing low over his eyes.

'Perfectly.' She didn't ask him why; didn't ask what made him hate the Funaro family so much. It was none of her business. 'Like I said, I'm not currently in the market for romance. For heaven's sake, look at my life!' She spread her arms wide. 'I think it's complicated enough without adding a romance to the mix, don't you?'

His lips twitched and it gave her hope that a sense of humour rested beneath that sober exterior. 'Perhaps,' he agreed.

She suddenly grinned. 'I'm a Funaro, and you're bad-tempered—it would be a most inauspicious match, don't you think? It will be much better to be colleagues, yes?'

He chuckled. '*Si*, this is true. Colleagues then. Come, let's shake on it.'

She placed her hand in his and they shook on it. Who knew? Maybe they'd even eventually become friends.

Audrey turned first one way and then the other in front of the mirror. Heavens! She eased back and twirled, only to discover her grandmother surveying her from the doorway.

She couldn't help but grin at the older woman. 'I did knock,' Marguerite said, 'but you obviously didn't hear me above that awful racket.' She pointed to Audrey's sound system.

Audrey immediately lowered the volume, but didn't turn it off. 'One day this summer, Grandmama, you and I are going to sip shandies out there on the terrace while I introduce you to the joy that is the music of Taylor Swift.'

'I will look forward to it,' Marguerite said with her customary poise, but Audrey could've sworn the older woman's eyes danced. 'In the meantime, you seem pleased with your new dress.'

She didn't just have a new dress. She had a whole new wardrobe! She'd never owned such beautiful clothes. Tonight she was to make her first appearance in public as a member of the family—at a lavish charity ball—and in its honour, Marguerite had commissioned this dress. Its folds of cream silk and pink lace made her look *beautiful*.

Or maybe that was the new hairstyle.

Or all of the makeup. She'd spent hours with a makeup artist being tutored in how to contour, shape and define each of her features. As if she were a painting or an embroidery—or a work of art.

'I feel like Cinderella,' she confided. Or Audrey Hepburn's character from *My Fair Lady*. On impulse she kissed the older woman's cheek. 'Does my appearance meet with your approval?'

'Yes.'

She'd discovered that her grandmother never gushed, but she also never lied about something as important to her as one's appearance. The hard knot at the centre of her that had been diminishing slowly over the past week eased further now. She wanted to do Marguerite proud, and tonight she meant to do exactly that. She'd be poised, polite and... Well, *polished* wasn't exactly the right word. Marguerite's level of polish came from having grown up in this world, and Audrey doubted she'd ever fully master it. But she'd be warm and kind, and she meant to enjoy every minute of the evening's festivities.

'Several other family members will be attending tonight.' She named two of Audrey's cousins and an uncle and his wife. 'And Gabriel, obviously.'

'Why *obviously*?' She hid a frown—rather well,

she thought. She'd get the hang of this poise thing yet. 'He doesn't strike me as…'

Marguerite raised an eyebrow.

'The social type.'

Gabriel had decreed they'd start her lessons next week, and other than her visit to his studio, she'd only seen him one other time this week when she and Lili had spent a happy couple of hours exploring the grounds, Lili showing Audrey all of her favourite spots on the estate. That was when she'd discovered Gabriel and Lili didn't have a suite in the villa, but stayed in a cottage on the grounds instead. He'd not spoken much; had spent more time trailing behind them than taking part in the conversation.

Maybe he'd been thinking about a project he was working on.

Or just ensuring she didn't get the wrong idea and start making big moon eyes at him.

'Gabriel is a patron of this particular charity. It's one that is close to his heart.'

Shame hit her then in a hot rush. She'd been so focused on her new dress and how she looked that she'd not given a second thought to what the charity might be. What charity were they supporting tonight? She was too embarrassed to ask Marguerite.

Swallowing, she made herself smile. 'Shall we all arrive together?'

'Good heavens, no, child.'

Child? She wanted to laugh. She was twenty-six!

'You and I shall take the car together, but we're going to arrive fashionably late.'

So they could make a splash? Her stomach started to churn.

'The others have made their own arrangements. Now remember, this evening all eyes will be upon you. You will keep your shoulders back and your chin high. You are a Funaro.'

She nodded.

'And you will meet me in the foyer no later than eight o'clock.'

'I won't be late.'

With a nod, the older woman left.

Turning back to the mirror, she stared at the unfamiliar reflection gazing back at her. She pointed at it. 'You can do this.' She'd do whatever necessary to make her grandmother, and the rest of the family, proud of her.

She was in the foyer at ten to eight. She suspected Marguerite wouldn't tolerate tardiness, and she'd rather be the one kept waiting. Besides, waiting was something she was used to.

A footstep on the stair above had her turning away from surveying her face in one of the many mirrors that dotted the wall. 'Gabriel.'

He stopped dead. His eyes widened and lips thinned.

Heat rose up her neck and across her cheeks.

She gestured to the mirror. 'I'm not usually so vain. I just can't believe what I look like.'

He didn't speak, but those grey eyes appraised her with a throbbing thoroughness that had her stomach clenching.

With an effort, she swallowed. 'I keep having to pinch myself to believe this is real.' She held out her inner arm to show him a red mark there. 'Which I better stop doing or I'll end up with a bruise.' And she doubted that'd meet with Marguerite's approval, either.

Gabriel stared at Audrey and couldn't utter a single damn word. At the back of his mind an ugly voice sounded: *And so it begins...* But his better self protested against the cynicism. Fina's fate didn't have to be Audrey's. It wasn't a foregone conclusion.

He was trying to protect himself. *Again.* Trying to avoid the soul-crushing disappointment of seeing another life wasted.

A hard knot squeezed his chest tight. If he'd tried harder with Fina—tried harder to break down her barriers, tried harder to make her see how self-destructive her behaviour had been— then maybe she'd be alive today and Lili would still have her mother.

He hadn't tried harder, though. He'd retreated to save himself from the pain of watching her drink herself into a stupor time and time again;

retreated from her rants and rages, and from the line of lovers she'd taken such pleasure in parading in front of him. He should've realised it had been a cry for help. Instead, he'd taken righteous refuge in hurt feelings, hurt pride and his sense of betrayal.

Did he mean to bury his head in the sand again now? Did he really mean to stand by and watch another woman be ruined by the Funaro fortune and do nothing?

Rolling his shoulders, he did what he could to shake off the thought.

'Stop looking at me like that.' Audrey pressed her hands to her stomach. 'You're making me nervous. At least tell me I'm going to pass muster.'

'You look very beautiful, but then I think you already know that.'

He did what he could to keep his voice measured. She *was* beautiful. But with her hair piled up on top of her head in a sophisticated updo that showed off the elegant line of her throat, and a dress that clung to curves that had his mouth drying, the skirt floating around her legs like a dream, a deep, hard lust fired to life inside him.

It had him wanting to throw his head back and howl. He'd desired women since Fina's death, had even slept with a few, but he'd not wanted anyone with the fire that pierced him now.

It was just clothes. His hands clenched. And makeup. And a fancy hairstyle. It should make no difference. But together, all of it brought to the fore her beauty, forcing him to acknowledge it…and feel the burn of need in his very bones. It meant he could no longer hide from it.

It was her simple delight, however, her astonishment at her appearance, that eventually burned away some of the hormonal mist. Her enjoyment was oddly touching, and he did not wish to dim it.

'And here I was hoping you'd be more eloquent.' She laughed, part amusement and part shamefaced embarrassment. 'Serves me right for being so frivolous.'

He forced himself down the last few steps. 'I meant what I said. You do look very beautiful.' To his relief, his voice emerged smooth and sincere. Her gaze moved over him like a gentle touch, and his skin tightened.

'You look very debonair yourself.'

The way she suddenly glanced away to fidget with an earring betrayed the fact that she, too, was aware of him. Her frown told him she was no more pleased about it than he was.

He stared at his feet. They were adults. They could ignore this.

She sent him a tight smile. 'But we both know beauty is as beauty does. Tonight's purpose isn't about me looking beautiful.'

It wasn't?

'But supporting a good cause, like breast cancer.'

His head came up. Did she care about such things?

'Marguerite gave me to understand it's an important one to you.'

'My mother died of breast cancer.'

'Oh, Gabriel, I didn't know. I'm sorry.'

He shrugged. 'It was a long time ago now.'

Nodding, she glanced up the stairs and then back at him, a question in her eyes.

'I wanted to see Lili settled in the nursery before I left. I had planned to leave before now, but she talked me into reading her a second bedtime story.'

That made her laugh, and a whole new awareness rippled over the surface of his skin. 'I didn't think, but of course she'd be staying here tonight.'

He didn't want to dwell on that. He knew Lili would come to no harm under Marguerite's roof. It's just he wanted, *needed*, to ensure that the Funaro influence didn't dominate Lili's life. He wanted his daughter to grow up to be whatever she wanted to be, not moulded into a cookie-cutter socialite with no anchor to keep her grounded. That lack of an anchor had destroyed Fina. He was determined Lili would find one in him, in the values he meant to instil in her, and in helping her find her purpose in life. He would do everything he could to protect her, to prevent her from feeling cast adrift, worthless and filled with despair.

'I understand we're travelling separately.'

Her frown had him chuckling. 'I suspect Marguerite will want to make a splash tonight as she introduces you to...'

She raised one marvellous eyebrow. 'Her friends?'

'High society.' He shoved his hands into the pockets of his trousers. 'And I prefer to drive myself. That way I can come and go as I please.'

An uncomfortable silence opened up then. 'You know everyone is going to want the inside story tonight. So...what's the party line?'

He'd be questioned, too, but he had the skills to deflect and the bad manners to tell people to mind their own business. Marguerite's high society only tolerated him because of his fame. He clenched his jaw so hard it started to ache. If he didn't find a way to unblock himself soon, though, he'd not have even that.

Beneath whatever perfume she wore, he still detected a note of lavender when she leaned towards him. 'The what?'

'How are you explaining the discovery that you're a Funaro heiress?'

Her lips turned down a fraction. 'Well, we're saying that my parents had an intense whirlwind affair. That resulted in...me. My father never knew my mother's true identity. She went off to see more of the world, with promises to come back, but never returned. As a result, I never knew I was a Funaro until my nonna's death when I received the letter she'd left for me.'

He wondered what the real story was. The one throbbing beneath the sanitised version. The shadows in her eyes told him there was one.

She leaned across and suddenly gripped his hand. 'I'm glad you're going to be there tonight, Gabriel. It'll help to have a friendly face in the crowd.'

Damn. Damn and blast!

He wasn't any kind of knight. Fina had proven that.

She smiled and it was as if the shadows had never been. 'I also plan to have fun this evening. In all my life, I've never been to a party like this one.'

He couldn't help feeling she was going to be sadly disappointed. And—

And nothing! She had her art. It would help when all of this tumbled down around her ears. It would be something she could fall back on. And that at least was something he could help her with.

CHAPTER FIVE

GABRIEL GLANCED AT his watch. It was nearing midnight and his gaze once more drifted across the dance floor to where Alessio Russo expertly spun Audrey around before pulling her flush against his body.

His grip tightened on his champagne flute. It was the second time Alessio had danced with Audrey this evening, and not the first time he'd pulled her in far too close. Nor was it the first time his hand had drifted lower than it ought to. Audrey again lifted the errant hand back to her waist.

Gabriel had kept a surreptitious eye on her all night. He'd told himself it was the least that he could do. She was a lamb in a room full of wolves, and what kind of person would he be if he simply abandoned her?

He glanced at Marguerite on the other side of the room. It'd make him no better than her or any of the other people here.

In contrast to them all, Audrey glowed like a soft candle at midnight, bathing all around her in warmth and welcome. It made things inside him ache. He wanted to march her off the dance floor and order her to keep her guard up around these people. He wanted—

Alessio's hand lowered to Audrey's backside once more. Gabriel knocked back the rest of his drink in a single gulp, set his glass to the nearest table and strode onto the dance floor. 'I believe I'm going to cut in.'

'But the song hasn't finished yet,' Alessio protested, 'and—'

Gabriel bared his teeth and Alessio hastily unhanded her. 'By all means.'

Audrey gurgled back a laugh as he fled and Gabriel took her in his arms. 'You've frightened the poor man half to death.'

As her hand curved in his and the other came to a rest on his shoulder, things that had been jarring all night suddenly eased. Audrey was warm and alive and those dancing eyes had a smile reluctantly tugging at his lips. 'Alessio is a sleaze. He deserves to be frightened half to death.'

'Ah, but apparently his family is of impeccable stock.'

No doubt that had come from Marguerite. A union between the Funaros and the Russos would be undeniably beneficial to Funaro business interests. He'd bet Marguerite hadn't mentioned that Alessio was also a gambler who was in debt up to his ears. *That* would be beside the point.

She waggled her eyebrows. 'Apparently, that's very important.'

'Tut-tut. Don't let Marguerite hear you speak so irreverently of bloodlines,' he scolded with mock sternness. But the vision of Alessio's hands on Audrey's hips, pulling her closer, rose through him once more and it was all he could do to not bare his teeth again. 'The Russos are an old and connected family, but you would think that, as such, they'd have taken the trouble to teach their children better manners. I know you were dealing with him as efficiently as you could in the circumstance, and I suspect you didn't want to make a scene by walking off the dance floor, but it hardly seemed fair you suffer those wandering hands a moment longer.'

'I appreciate the intervention. I think he'd had a little too much to drink.'

Dio. Must this woman always make excuses for bad behaviour?

'And it's nice to dance with you, Gabriel. For once, I don't have to make small talk, sidestep impertinent questions and pretend to be…' She trailed off, but he knew what she meant.

'So Cinderella isn't enjoying the ball as much as she thought she would?'

'Oh, no, I am! I'm having the most exciting time.'

She was?

'The dinner was a revelation—I mean, *caviar.* Before tonight I'd never had French champagne, either.'

'And did you like them both?'

She nodded, those warm walnut eyes dancing. 'As my father would say, I've champagne tastes on a beer budget.'

An uncharacteristic snort shot from him, making several people glance around at him in surprise.

'What does your father think about all of this?'

When her face fell, he wished he'd not asked.

'Well, I only told him this week. Once I realised it was going to make the papers. He was a bit…shocked.'

He could imagine. Had the man really been in ignorance of Danae's true identity as a Funaro?

'But he's recently remarried and has started a new job in the States, and it's keeping him very busy, so he won't have much time to worry.'

'Speaking of marriage… Did he and Danae marry?'

'My dear Gabriel, you're definitely going off script with that question.'

He didn't know if her chiding was serious or not.

'Apparently, the right response is *my parents had a fiery affair.*'

Marguerite's hand again, no doubt.

She bit her lip. 'I always thought they had, but maybe I was wrong.'

Or maybe…

'But if they were, it clearly wasn't legal.'

Because Danae had never divorced from her first husband.

'Nobody talks of her, you know?'

Of Danae? Of course, they didn't. And he had no intention of talking out of school, either.

Before he realised it, they'd danced another dance, and he grew aware of the speculation growing rife in the eyes of those who surreptitiously but greedily watched. *Damn.* He didn't want to be the subject of that kind of gossip or—

Though… He glanced down at the woman in his arms. Perhaps it wouldn't hurt for people to think he was interested. It'd help keep the worst of the fortune hunters and those who wanted to use her for other kinds of gains—for family and business alliances, but who wouldn't care about her as a living, breathing person—at bay.

'More champagne?'

She gave a funny little shimmy as the dance came to an end. 'Yes, please. Who knew dancing could build such a thirst?'

After seizing two champagnes from a passing waiter, he led her to one of the chairs arranged at intervals around the dance floor.

She patted the chair beside her. 'Don't loom, Gabriel. Sit.'

He was used to the women at these events who wanted to cultivate his company by raising flirtatious eyebrows and sending him long, lingering glances. Or, alternately, giving a prim thank-you as their eyes scanned the crowd for someone more biddable and civilised.

Audrey did neither of those things and as her

smile informed him she was enjoying his company, he sat, then watched as an expression of bliss crossed her face when she sipped her champagne. He sipped his, too, taking the time to focus on the spark and fizz. She was right. The wine was excellent.

When had it all become old hat to him? When had he started to take it for granted? When had he started hating it?

The answer came swiftly and surely: *Since Fina died.*

'Excuse me, sir, but Ms Marguerite Funaro asked me to give you a message.'

He glanced at the uniformed waiter who appeared at his elbow. 'Yes?'

'She had a headache and has retired early. She requested you see Ms Martinelli safely home.'

'Thank you.' He did what he could not to betray his surprise.

When the man moved away, Audrey frowned. 'Are you sure Marguerite warned you off? Are you sure she's not trying her hand at some kind of surreptitious matchmaking?'

He couldn't help it. He laughed. 'I'm certain.'

She blew out a breath. 'Good.'

He rolled his shoulders, tried to dislodge an odd itch. 'Why?'

'Because you told me you hate to be manipulated. And while the motives might be benevolent, I suspect you would hate someone trying to set you up.'

Benevolent? Dear God, this woman! 'I am certain your grandmother is not trying to set us up.'

'In that case…' She took her phone from her clutch and composed a text message. No doubt telling her grandmother that she hoped she was feeling better soon. When she was done, she turned back to him. 'Is it my imagination, or does the room sit up and take notice whenever I dance more than one dance with a partner?'

'It's not your imagination.'

'So the fact we just danced two and a half dances have set tongues wagging?'

'*Si.*'

Her pleated brow told him what she thought of that.

'Were you being honest with me when you said you were not currently interested in finding yourself a husband or having a romance?'

Those walnut eyes flashed. 'Of course I was.'

He liked her all the more for the fire. 'In that case, I apologise.'

'Eventually, I'd like to fall in love, marry…have children.' She shrugged. 'But it's the farthest thing from my mind at the moment. There's just too much to learn and come to grips with.' She bit her lip. 'I don't…'

He raised his brows.

She leaned a little closer. 'I don't wish to make the same mistakes my mother clearly did.'

Her words chilled him to the bone. He didn't want that for her, either. He *could* help. A little. 'In that case, what harm will it do if people do link us romantically?'

Her eyes grew comically wide.

The more he thought about it, the more the notion recommended itself to him. If everyone thought he and Audrey were dating, it would give her time to find her feet and work out who she could trust and who to keep her distance from.

'Are you suggesting we *lie*?'

'Absolutely not. *We* don't lie, remember? But very few people will ask the question outright. If they do, you can deny it.' They wouldn't believe her, but he kept that piece of information to himself. 'In the meantime, it will buy you time, and give you an excuse to refuse all the invitations single eligible men are going to start sending your way.'

'You think men are going to start asking me on dates?'

'I don't think, I know.'

She sipped her champagne. 'I don't want to go on dates.'

'See? My plan is pure brilliance.'

That made her laugh. 'Won't it cramp your style?'

'I am not currently interested in dating, either.'

'Why not?'

Things inside him clenched. 'I need to focus on my art and my daughter. I do not have room for other things.'

She looked as if she wanted to say something, but eventually shrugged. 'Okay.'

Her easy acceptance made him want to laugh.

'If you're going to be my lift home tonight, I want you to know I'm happy to leave the party whenever you are. Please don't change your plans to suit me. But if I don't at least sample that chocolate mousse before we leave, I'm going to regret it for the rest of my life.'

He stared at her. 'You are very easy to be with. Do you know that?'

She blinked.

'You are not—what do they say?—high-maintenance.' All the women he knew were high-maintenance.

'Low-maintenance, that's me.' She grinned. 'Apparently, I'm obliging to a fault.'

'Then I will oblige you in my turn and get you one of those chocolate mousses.'

'And then will you tell me how one goes about setting up a foundation like the one you have for your mother?'

He stared at her for a long moment, but those cinnamon-spice eyes stared back at him unfazed. What on earth was she up to? 'If you wish.'

'Thank you.'

* * *

'Which do you like better? The pink or white marshmallows?' Lili asked.

'I like the white ones best.' Audrey reached into the bowl, took a white marshmallow and popped it into her mouth.

Gabriel pretended to be immersed in his sketch—which was a joke in itself, but not one that was funny. He glared at the rose he was supposed to be sketching. It didn't speak to him at all. Maybe one of the Madonna lilies would be more suitable. He stared at the nearest one, but although it was perfection, not a ripple of enthusiasm lifted through him. Instead, his attention remained on his daughter and her aunt. They were currently stretched out on the blanket on the lawn in this sheltered corner of the garden. It was a corner few people came to, which is why he'd chosen it.

'But the pink marshmallows are *so* much prettier!'

'They are prettier, but I think the white ones taste nicer.'

He thought they tasted exactly the same. Clearly, Audrey held a contrary view on the matter.

Lili reached for a white marshmallow, then, just like Audrey had, and he bit back a smile.

'It's like clothes,' Audrey said, turning onto her back and pointing to a cloud. 'That one looks like a rabbit.'

For the briefest of moments, he imagined lying

above her, staring down at her. Imagined the feel of her body; imagined the silken nakedness of her and—

Dio! He tried to banish the picture from his mind.

Lili, in perfect imitation of Audrey, lay on her back, too. 'What do you mean marshmallows are like clothes?'

'Well, Grandmama has insisted on buying me a lot of beautiful new clothes for all the balls and dinner parties and luncheons I'll be attending. And some of them are *so* beautiful. But you want to know what my favourite item of clothing is?'

Lili stared at her with wide eyes. 'What?'

'My really old jeans that I've had for a million years. I mean I know all the pretty clothes look nicer, but they're nowhere near as comfortable.' She sat up. 'Can you keep a secret?' Her eyes danced and he found himself as entranced as Lili. 'Grandmama told the maid to throw my old jeans away, but I sneaked out to the bin and retrieved them.'

Lili clapped her hands over her mouth, but girlish giggles still escaped.

'But you can't tell Grandmama! Promise?'

'I promise!'

And then Lili threw herself at Audrey, who caught her as if it was the most natural thing in the world, and who hugged her back with what looked like her entire being.

CHAPTER SIX

AUDREY'S ART LESSONS officially started the week following her society debut. Gabriel had insisted on three lessons a week—and by lessons he meant whole days spent at the studio working. It hadn't been a suggestion, more a command, but Audrey hadn't argued because, a) he was doing her a favour, and b) she wasn't used to having so much free time on her hands and she'd started to find herself searching for things to do.

Something beyond trying to work out the tangled tensions and strange undercurrents among the various Funaro family members.

They were nothing like her family back home in Melbourne. Surely, money and social standing shouldn't change family dynamics *that* much. She suddenly wished she'd taken her cousin Frankie up on her offer to come to Lake Como for moral support. Frankie was currently holidaying in Tuscany, and she had the ability to cut through nonsense and get to the heart of a matter.

Blowing out a breath, she told herself to stop being a baby. But that didn't stop the warning her grandmother had given her last night and the promise she'd extracted from weighing heavily on her shoulders.

Glancing across at Gabriel, who scowled with savage intensity at a half-finished sculpture, she had to suppress a shiver. He looked every bit as ferocious as Marguerite had claimed.

Does he, though?

Cocking her head to one side, she studied him more carefully. Maybe he was tired. Maybe he was wrestling with his muse and not happy with the way his work was going. Maybe he just had a headache.

A pulse pounded in her throat. Maybe Marguerite had misjudged him.

Chilly grey eyes lifted to hers with remarkable precision, as if aware she'd been surveying him. 'You've not managed a single stitch in the last thirty minutes.'

She shrugged and gestured at his sculpture. 'You haven't made any progress in the last thirty minutes, either.'

'I'm cogitating. What's your excuse?'

She was brooding. Not that she had any intention of telling him so. 'I'm just getting used to my new surroundings.'

'Did you have this same kind of trouble when you were working with Madame De Luca?'

No. But that was before her life had been turned upside down.

'I didn't think so.' Slamming hands to his hips, he let out an insultingly impatient breath. 'And you worked fine on Monday and Wednesday. Tell me what's bothering you.'

And just like that, without warning, anger

flared. Anger she suspected she'd been tamping down for four long years. 'Stop ordering me about like some damn maidservant!'

He blinked.

She was so damn tired of being the good girl, the responsible one, the person who never rocked the boat; the one who always bent over backwards to make sure everyone else felt comfortable. Nobody here cared if she felt uncomfortable or out of her depth or *anything*. Why did she always feel as if she had to be the one to make up the shortfall?

A different expression took up residence in those grey eyes, but it wasn't one she could read. Swallowing, she waited for the customary guilt to hit her—to make her feel bad for stepping outside the lines she normally prescribed for herself. And kept right on waiting.

She let out a breath she hadn't realised she'd been holding. Maybe here in this extraordinary studio the normal rules didn't apply. It was a freeing thought.

Perfect lips pursed. 'I see we're not going to have the usual kind of teacher-student relationship.'

'I have a feeling sitting at your feet and staring adoringly up at you isn't the way to earn your respect.'

'And you want my respect?'

'Don't we all want to be respected?'

And liked?

She had a feeling, though, that Gabriel didn't care whether people liked him or not.

'It's more important to respect ourselves before we start worrying what other people think of us.' He folded his arms and widened his stance. 'I didn't mean to sound so abrupt before. I apologise if you felt I was ordering you about. I'm not used to having anyone else other than Lili in the studio.'

All of her righteous outrage dissolved at his words.

'However, I would honestly like to know what's bothering you.'

She glanced at his work in progress and then back up at him. 'I'd like to know what's bothering you, too.' She was tired of being the only one who felt clueless, the only one who felt vulnerable.

He pulled in a long breath that had already broad shoulders broadening and a deep chest deepening, and something inside her quickened. Swallowing, she forced her gaze back to his, refusing to notice anything else.

He stared at her for a long moment. 'What's said in the studio stays in the studio?'

She pondered that then nodded. 'Okay.'

He gestured at his sculpture. 'I'm blocked. I have been for months. Eight months to be precise.'

Her jaw dropped.

'It's not something I'd like made public. I have three commissions due by the end of the year and yet… I have nothing.' That dark scowl bloomed across his face again. 'It's beyond frustrating and makes me testy.'

She couldn't think of a single word to say.

'No platitudes to offer?'

His sarcasm, she finally saw, was a shield. It wasn't directed at her personally, but at himself. She lifted a hand and let it drop. 'I'm sorry, of course, but that's hardly helpful.'

He rolled his shoulders. 'Any advice to offer?'

'Me?'

'Yes, of course you.' That scowl became ferocious again. 'Why not you? You're an artist, aren't you?'

That was debatable. She stared at the screen in front of her, at her barely started embroidery, and forced her chin up. 'You said you've been blocked for eight months. Did something happen eight months ago?' Had he suffered a trauma or an accident? 'Have you been ill or anything?'

'No.' He was silent for a moment. 'You've never suffered from a creative block?'

'I've never had the opportunity. I've only ever worked on my embroideries in my free time and in stolen moments.'

Perfect lips twisted. 'So I'm wallowing in my malcontent and wasting the good fortune I've been given. Being self-indulgent.'

'That's not what I said!' But it's how he saw himself, she realised. 'I think you need to relax

a bit and stop being so tense.' *And judgemental.*
'Coffee?'

She didn't wait for an answer, but strode across
to the small kitchenette and the coffee machine,
glancing up briefly at the mysterious mezzanine
level that hadn't been part of her tour, before busy-
ing herself making coffee. 'When was the last
time you made something just for fun? Just because you wanted to?'

'I...'

She looked at him. Could he not remember?
'I've fitted my embroideries in between work and
other things. It has always been a form of relax-
ation and play.' *That had to change once it became
your day job.*

'What other things?'

She glanced around at the unexpected question.
For a moment she was tempted to tell him, but
Marguerite would hate it if she did. Marguerite
had requested Audrey not tell anyone.

Ice slid in between her ribs. Her sister Johanna
wasn't anything to be ashamed of. She'd reluctantly agreed not to mention her twin in the near
future, though. She wanted a chance for her and
Marguerite to grow close, before putting forward
the memorial she had in mind for her sister.

She busied herself with the coffee again. 'Oh,
you know. Family and taking care of a house and
chores and all the other things normal people do.'

He ambled across to lean on a kitchen bench. 'You do not consider the Funaros normal people?'

His lips had lifted in a smile, humour lurking in his eyes, making him look younger, and she shook her head, battling a strange sense of breath-lessness. 'I do not. I doubt they'd know the first thing about keeping a house clean or how to do the grocery shopping or put on a load of laundry.'

His warm chuckle lifted the fine hairs on her arms.

'Do you?' The question blurted out of her un-bidden, and he sobered.

'I grew up in a working-class family. My father died when I was young and my mother was an in-valid. More often than not, the household chores fell to me. As I suspect they did to you, too, if your father was a scientist. I take it that it was his house that you kept.'

She'd always thought it was hers, too. Just for a moment their gazes caught and clung. Shaking herself, she poured coffee into two mugs. 'I be-lieve it's called character building.'

He gave another of those rare chuckles that threatened to wrap around her like a warm blanket.

Don't think about warm blankets. Or rumpled sheets.

Straightening, she forced her mind back to their conversation. 'What I'm trying to say is that em-broidery has always been my escape from the real world.' She handed him a mug. 'I've never been commissioned to make something for someone else. I mean, I've made gifts for family members and friends, but I've never had to make something to measure like you. Things have to change when art becomes your work.'

'It does not feel like work. To be able to make a living from my art has been a joy.'

It was hard to associate joy and Gabriel in the same sentence.

'Is that what has been worrying you? That you now have to share your art? Is that why you haven't been able to work this morning?' His eyes narrowed, and he shook his head. 'No, that is not it.' He shrugged when she sent him an exasperated glare. 'What? You have an expressive face.'

'Then I'm going to need lessons in how to look like a closed book.'

'That is something I can help you with, too.'

She might just take him up on it. 'Yesterday afternoon Marguerite called me into her private apartment for a chat.'

His mouth flattened. 'Come, let's get some fresh air.'

He led her outside to the wooden table and benches that rested on one side of the studio. With the sun warm on her face, she sank down to a bench to gobble up the expansive views of unruffled water in various shades of silver, deep blue and navy green that spread before her. Timeless mountains rising silent and majestic all around.

'What did Marguerite say that still has you chafing a day later?'

She snapped back with a bump. 'She warned me off you.'

His face became enviously unreadable, and she swallowed. 'Remember what we agreed. What's said in the studio stays in the studio.'

'Absolutely.'

She bit her lip. 'Are you offended?'

She'd love to somehow bridge the uncomfortable gap that existed between Marguerite and Gabriel. It'd be far more pleasant for Lili if her father and grandmother could be friends. And Lili *was* her niece. She'd do all she could to ensure the little girl was happy and content.

'Why should I be offended? As you know, she has already given me that same lecture.'

It wasn't an answer.

'Marguerite is always scheming, though. I do not trust her.'

Marguerite had likewise been far from flattering about Gabriel. She'd said that he wasn't to be trusted where women were concerned; that he'd become too angry and embittered after Serafina's death—as if he wanted revenge on the entire female population.

Revenge? Because no woman could ever live up to his memory of Serafina? The thought had made her stomach churn.

Marguerite had said she didn't want to see Audrey suffer at his hands. Audrey didn't want that, either.

'She made me promise to not fall in love with you.'

He shot to his feet. 'And you *agreed* to such an archaic directive?'

Those grey eyes glared at her, his large body bristling with outrage, but he didn't alarm her. Not anymore. She'd seen beneath the bluster. Whatever Gabriel wanted her and the rest of the world to think of him—and, again, she doubted he cared—she knew that beneath that bristling demeanour, he was a good man.

Wasn't he helping her with her art? And hadn't he rescued her on Saturday night when Alessio's hands had been straying? And the fact his daughter adored him spoke volumes. Yes, Gabriel Dimarco, despite whatever Marguerite thought, was a good man.

She lifted her chin and glared back at him. 'Of course I did. I thought you'd be pleased.'

His mouth worked but not a single sound emerged.

'Why all this outrage? Didn't you demand the same promise from me? On this one issue, at least, you and Marguerite seem to be in complete agreement.'

And so was she. He might be a good man, but to fall in love with him...

She went cold all over. She hadn't been enough

for her mother and she hadn't been enough for her father. She wasn't making the mistake of falling in love with Gabriel, because she'd never be enough for him, either—not enough for him to overcome his prejudices; not enough for him to be a part of a family he loathed; not enough for him to risk getting his heart burned again. No, she was nowhere near enough for him on any level.

All she was good for was as an aunt to his daughter. One he could trust to be sensible. And that was something. She knew that. But it was a line drawn in the sand...and he wasn't even totally convinced she could be that person yet, either. She suppressed a shudder, imagining what it would be like to give your heart to such a man. He'd shred it. Oh, he wouldn't mean to, but his coldness, his inflexibility, his indifference... It would be the chilliest, loneliest of prisons.

Not going to happen.

Nonna had taught her that comfort and strength came in the shape of family. Her parents might've let her down, but her sister, grandmother, aunt and her cousin had all been there for her. She'd find strength and solace in her new family. *That* was where she needed to focus her efforts.

Gabriel stared at Audrey and wanted to yell; wanted to slash dark, ugly colour across a canvas. It made no sense. He had extracted the same promise. Why should it infuriate him that Marguerite would request it, too?

Because it was none of Marguerite's business who he dated or slept with.

'On Saturday night, when she saw how ably you rescued me from Mr Wandering Hands, she wanted to make sure I didn't read too much into your gallantry.'

His hand had clenched on the table beside his mug. He forced it to unclench. 'Why, then, when she could have the finest and most celebrated teachers here with a click of her fingers, would she entrust me with your artistic instruction?'

She leaned towards him as if he was hard of hearing…or slow of understanding. 'She said you are one of the most important artists of your generation. She knows what a coup it is that you've taken an interest in my education.' She folded her hands in her lap like a prim schoolgirl. 'I've been ordered to learn all I can from you.' Lovely lips twitched. 'And to not make a nuisance of myself.'

His eyes practically started from his head. 'I do not believe you.'

An eyebrow rose, but laughter still remained in the depths of those spice-coloured eyes.

'Sorry, that was a figure of speech, of disbelief, not an accusation. I know you do not lie.'

Her eyes abruptly dropped and a burning started in his chest. What wasn't she telling him? Had Marguerite told her he was a beast where women were concerned—that he used and abused his paramours before discarding them with nary a thought?

As far as the Funaros were concerned, he had never been good enough for their darling Serafina. And now he clearly wasn't good enough for their darling Audrey, either.

A sigh escaped soft lips, and things inside him tightened as his gaze fixed on those lips. Dear God, he had to stop fixating on them—their shape and texture—and wondering what it would be like to kiss them. Wondering what kind of lover Audrey would be—would she be shy or bold? He thought she would be shy, but he suspected there was fire banked beneath that unflappable exterior and he'd—

Stop!

'What's the issue between you and Marguerite anyway?' Her brow pleated. 'Is it to do with Serafina?'

He stiffened at his wife's name.

She huffed out a laugh. 'Bingo. Nobody wants me to ask questions, but this is my family. I don't understand what happened or why this has made everyone the way they are.'

'And how do you think they are?'

She stared out at the lake, rubbed a hand across her chest. 'Broken,' she finally said.

The single word made him flinch. So did the

sorrow in her gaze—all this concern for these people she barely yet knew.

'Nobody speaks of either Serafina or Danae. As soon as I mention either name, the conversation is deftly changed to some other channel or people excuse themselves, because there's something that they have to *see to immediately*. If a long-lost daughter turned up to meet my family in Australia, we'd regale her with all the stories we could about the mother she'd never known… and the sister.'

He silently swore.

'Obviously, the stories are far from pretty. Obviously, they're painful. But I don't see how keeping me in the dark is going to help.'

'I suspect Marguerite is wanting you to get used to everything else before subjecting you to the less salubrious side of the family history.'

Firm eyes met his. She might appear meek and quiet on first meeting, but there was a surprising strength to this woman, too. 'What's the deal between you and Marguerite?' she asked again.

Things inside him clenched and burned. 'Marguerite holds me responsible for Fina's death.'

Her face fell.

'While I hold *her* responsible.' She opened her mouth, but he held up a hand. 'No more for today.'

With a nod, she transferred her gaze to her coffee. 'Can I ask a side question, then? Why do you spend the summers here on Marguerite's estate?'

'Lili. It is an arrangement made between lawyers, to give her the opportunity to know her mother's family. Marguerite could insist that I drop Lili off and leave her here, but we both know Lili will be happier if I am here, too. So Marguerite tolerates me. In return, I allow her visits throughout the rest of the year.'

The smallest of smiles touched those lips.

Don't notice the lips.

'You've found a way to work together—for Lili's sake.'

'If I had my way, Lili would have no contact at all with the Funaro family.'

She frowned. 'You have to believe it's only right that she knows both sides of her family—'

'No, I don't!'

He couldn't help the savagery with which he spat out those words. He hated himself for them when Audrey flinched, but he couldn't take them back. They were the truth. 'The Funaro family are poison.' And with everything he had, he wished he could protect Lili from them.

Her eyes throbbed into his. 'You hate them.'

He normally kept a more civilised facade on these emotions, but Audrey had somehow prised that lid off and it was taking all of his strength to hold them in check.

'I'm a Funaro. Do you hate me, too?'

Exhaustion overtook him then. 'I do not hate you, Audrey. You are not a true Funaro. You are,

I suspect, very much a Martinelli.' And his hate was not so illogical.

Are you sure?

Of course he was sure. He loathed the Funaros for not believing the rules applied to them, for thinking themselves above the laws that defined and governed normal behaviour—for their excesses and entitlement and selfishness.

'There's something I don't understand.'

He frowned. 'Just the one?'

'Why *have* you agreed to take my artistic education in hand if you hate the family so much?'

The way she said *hate* made him sound like a monster. And who knows? Maybe that was exactly what he'd become. If he'd managed to corral his anger and resentment towards Fina, she might still be here. And Lili might still have her mother.

'Lili.' The single word cracked from lips that didn't want to cooperate, but he suddenly and desperately didn't want this woman to let his daughter down the way her mother had. He would do everything in his power to prevent that, regardless of what he thought of the rest of the Funaro family.

'Lili?'

She said his daughter's name with such affection. Nodding, he rubbed a hand over his face. 'She adores you.'

'I adore her, too.'

'Do you know what she said to me the other

night? She said that she loved you and that she was certain her mother would be just like you.'

Audrey gave a funny little hiccup, her eyes growing suspiciously bright.

'And then she asked me if you were going to die like her mother had died.'

The soft gasp speared to the very centre of him.

'The Funaro women sometimes self-destruct, Audrey. It is what they do. It is what your mother did and it is what your sister did. Nobody talks of it because it brought shame and scandal to the Funaro name—and that is something that Marguerite finds unforgivable.'

She stared at him for a long moment. 'The reason Marguerite doesn't talk of them is because their deaths hurt her too much. She loved them and it hurts her to remember how they died.'

'You are seeing what you want to see. You only see the best in people.'

'While you only see their worst.'

She didn't say it as an accusation. Just sadly, as if she felt bad for him. An itch settled between his shoulder blades. 'I did not see what was happening to Fina. I didn't realise how close she was skating to the edge. Marguerite did not see it, either.'

'And as a result, you blame each other.'

He ignored that. 'Fina had nothing to fall back on—no resources beyond partying ever harder and trying an ever-greater array of drugs.'

He watched her digest that.

And lovers. Fina had also taken lovers. Lots of them. He left that unsaid, though. Even now Fina's infidelity chafed at him. He'd have given her everything, but she hadn't wanted anything he'd had to offer.

All she'd wanted was to annoy her grandmother by marrying someone none of them considered suitable. He'd been nothing but Fina's act of rebellion, and the knowledge left a bitter taste in his mouth. He'd been too focused on getting a divorce, and custody of Lili, to see how far down Fina was spiralling.

He leaned towards Audrey now. If he had any say in the matter, this woman would not follow Fina's path. 'Your art will give you something to fall back on—somewhere to escape to when the pressures of life in the fast lane, the pressure of being a Funaro, become too much. I do not want you to let Lili down the way Fina let her down.'

'Oh, God, Gabriel…'

She stared at him, stricken. Reaching out, she gripped his forearm, her hand small and pale against his tanned skin. 'I am *not* a life-in-the-fast-lane person.'

'Not yet.'

'And I am *never* going to take drugs.'

'So you say now, but how can you be so certain?'

'Because I care about my health!'

She was a nurse's aide. She must've seen what drugs did to people.

'Do you take drugs? Or do you mean to in the future?'

He stiffened. 'Absolutely not!'

She glanced to where her hand rested on his arm, as if his muscles tensing beneath her fingertips was a fascinating sensation. He flexed his arm again. The action involuntary. Her fingers firmed against him as if to test the solidity of the flesh beneath... And then she snapped away as if he burned her. The way she swallowed and glanced out at the lake had his every primal instinct firing to life.

Audrey found him attractive. And he found satisfaction in that knowledge. A deep, burning satisfaction. If he turned her face towards him, would she let him kiss her? If he kissed her with the deep, thorough hunger pouring through him now, would she kiss him back with the same abandon? Would she wrap her arms around him and press herself against him in a silent plea for more?

His breath sawed in and out of his lungs. Would she let him peel the clothes from her body and lose himself in the—

What the hell...?

This woman was off-limits. No matter how much he might wonder what it would be like to bed her, it was not a fantasy in which he could indulge. For Lili's sake. For Audrey's sake, too.

And his own.

She turned with eyes that seemed to shine with

some powerful inner light. 'You've agreed to take charge of my education because you want to protect me.'

'Do not look at me like that.' He pointed a shaking finger at her. He was not a knight in shining armour.

'Like what?'

'Like I am a hero.' The idea was laughable.

'You said I like to see the best in people.'

'You will be foolish to see what isn't there.'

'Or maybe you need to start seeing yourself through eyes like mine.'

This woman had no idea, and she would be hurt, and hurt badly, if this was the way she meant to deal with the Funaros.

'I fear for you, Audrey, but I will not be drawn back into that world—the one the Funaros inhabit.'

'That sounds like a warning.'

It was. 'Why is this family so important to you?'

She folded her arms. 'Why is Lili so important to you?'

He waved that off. A child was an altogether different thing. He thought back to the things that she'd told him. 'Your nonna recently died,' he started slowly, 'and your father has abandoned you for pastures greener.'

'He hasn't abandoned me!' But her gaze slid away.

'It was his house that you kept. This I know already. You told me as much. No doubt you cooked and cleaned for him.' Cared for him.

She shrugged, but a new tension threaded through her. 'It was my home, too. It was the family home.'

His heart started to thump. She'd said her father had taken a new job in America. 'Audrey, what happened to the family home?'

She moistened her lips, not meeting his eyes. 'It was sold.'

Dio! No wonder she felt so lost, so rootless. But to pin her hopes on the Funaros… 'You are lonely, feeling at a loose end. And are now hoping this new family you've discovered will fill the holes in your life and your heart.'

She turned to him fully, a frown in her eyes. 'I want to love them and I want them to love me.' She touched a hand to her chest. 'I want to belong. What's so wrong with that?'

'The Funaros are not that kind of family.'

'So says you, and you clearly don't want to belong to anyone. You'll have to excuse me if I take what you say on the subject with a grain of salt.'

'You want them to save you. When they cannot even save themselves. You will be disappointed and disillusioned and—'

'Let's agree to disagree on that one. Or we'll have an awful falling out and I'd prefer that we didn't.'

He'd prefer that, too.

'Do you ever sketch, Gabriel?'

The change in topic threw him. 'Yes, of course.' He made multiple sketches of his sculptures before starting them.

'Me, too. I want to sit on that rock over there and sketch out a design that's started to come to me. I want to somehow try and capture all this.' She gestured at the view.

'Very well. And once you are done you can explain your process to me.'

'Okay, but fair's fair. You need to sketch, too, and explain your process to me.'

He didn't have a process at the moment. He had nothing!

Which meant he didn't have anything to lose, either. 'Very well. I will remain here and try to capture the mountains.'

Fifteen minutes later he gave up with an exasperated sigh. Glancing across at Audrey, who sat on her rock at the other end of the small bay, he found her with head bent over her sketchpad. Picking up a charcoal, he drew a few lines to make the shape of her. Audrey was an interesting combination of frailty and strength. And as the clash between weakness and strength was what he often took as his subject...

Frowning, he drew a few more lines. And then some more. Before he knew it, his hand was flying across the page.

CHAPTER SEVEN

GABRIEL'S STICK OF CHARCOAL raced across the page of his sketchpad as if afraid that if it didn't keep moving, the image it was trying to capture would disappear and fade to black.

Audrey wanted to go peer over his shoulder, curious to see what had finally sparked his creativity, but didn't dare disturb him. Instead, she sat on the nearby rustic retaining wall with her sketchpad in her lap and remained silent.

A breath of warm air fanned the hair at her nape and a beetle negotiated the grass and pebbles at her feet. She watched its progress, but Gabriel's earlier words continued to go around and around in her mind.

You want them to save you when they cannot even save themselves.

Her heart pounded. She'd never felt so seen— so *judged*. Was that what she wanted—for them to save her?

Losing Nonna had made her realise that there were only Aunt Deidre, Frankie and herself left of her family. Oh, she'd still have her father, but while he'd been physically present, he'd been as absent as her mother in all the ways that had counted. But if anything were to happen to Aunt Deidre or Frankie…

Her mouth dried. Did she really hope the Funaros would fill that gap?

They cannot even save themselves.

She pulled her gaze from the beetle and stared out at the water. Maybe she could do something about that. She wasn't weak and she wasn't pathetic. Her heart was big enough and strong enough to take a few knocks if the prize at the end was a family that loved each other, that pulled together.

She'd had that with Nonna and Johanna, and Frankie and Aunt Deidre. There was absolutely no reason why she couldn't have it with Marguerite and Lili and the rest of the Funaro family as well. She had no intention of replacing one family with another, but she could widen her circle. And it wasn't a one-way street. She'd be gaining them, but they'd be gaining her, too.

Something trilled a pretty melody from a nearby tree. As she turned to try and spot the culprit, she realised the scratching of the charcoal had ceased and Gabriel now stared at her, brows lowering over his eyes.

'When did you move?' The frown deepened. 'In my mind's eye you've been on that little headland for the last hour.'

She shrugged. 'Time seems to move differently here. But probably twenty minutes ago.'

He shook himself, patted the table. 'Come. Let me see your sketches.'

She moved to the seat opposite. 'May I see yours?'

He hesitated, but with the smallest of shrugs, nodded. They exchanged sketchpads.

His was still open to the final sketch he'd done. Glancing down, her mouth dried. Turning the pages over, she followed them back to the first of his drawings before returning to the last one, her heart pounding. She knew he watched, and the weight of his stare did strange things to her insides. Moistening her lips, she tried to find something to say.

'What do you think?'

She didn't know if her opinion mattered to him or not. 'They're all of me,' she blurted out.

'Yes.'

He gave no explanation, his face giving nothing away. But… What did it mean? Why would he draw her? Why would he find her so fascinating?

Just like the sculpture in Como that had enthralled her, one couldn't tell if the figure on the rock—*her*—would remain there strong and steadfast, or whether the water would rise up to engulf it.

'It is important for you to develop an artistic sensibility. What do you think of it objectively?'

She forced herself to focus on the overall impact of the sketch—the strong lines, the ambiguity… Its strange beauty. 'Because the subject is me, and I've never been the subject for a work of art before, it's hard to be objective. This is only a sketch, but it has a real impact. It feels…alive.'

He took the sketchpad from her and surveyed it with narrowed eyes. 'Yes.' He nodded. 'This is something I can work with.'

'Why?'

He glanced up.

'Why me?'

One broad shoulder lifted. 'I was sketching the mountains, but they bored me. And then I saw you and there was something about your posture that caught my attention. Before I knew it, I was trying to capture it in a sketch…and then sketching as if my life depended on it.'

A thrill shook her to her very core. Something about her fascinated him. To think that a man like Gabriel would find someone like her captivating… She hugged the knowledge close. Very slowly, however, the excitement drained away. The water in the drawing, so still, somehow evoked a quiet menace that threatened both woman and rock.

Some Funaros self-destruct.

That was the subject of the sketch. He feared she'd follow in the footsteps of her mother and sister. He had no faith that her strength would prevail over whatever innate weakness he thought resided in her blood. He was recording a downfall that may not happen.

A downfall that *wouldn't* happen!

Lifting her chin, she glared at him. His eyes flashed with brief amusement, before he closed his sketchpad and slapped hers on top of it. Flicking through the various sketches, his lips pursed, his gaze halting only briefly on the final drawing. Eventually, he handed it back to her. 'It will make a pretty piece.'

She blinked. 'That sounds dismissive.' What was wrong with pretty?

'Pretty has its place.'

That sounded even more dismissive. 'But?'

Leaning back, he folded his arms and it drew her attention to the rock-hard strength of his chest. She swallowed, a pulse at the centre of her starting to pound. He'd taken her as his subject, and now all she could think about was if she had the skill to commit all of that raw masculinity to an embroidery—capture it in linen, silk and wool. To wonder what it would be like to draw close enough to touch all of that raw power.

Her pulse pounded harder, making it difficult to draw breath. What would it be like to press herself against such a body? Watch as that body rippled with awareness of a feminine presence— a feminine presence that could fire it to life and exhort it to—

Dear God!

Dragging her gaze back to his face, she found those merciless eyes watching her with a narrowed chill. Had he read her thoughts? Recognised her desires? If he had, the chill in his expression told her it wasn't an attraction he reciprocated.

Heat flooded her face.

Channel Marguerite.

With an effort, she kept her chin high. Women must find Gabriel attractive all the time. It didn't have to mean anything.

She *had* to keep her guard up. For heaven's sake, he was waiting for her downfall. He didn't want it to happen, and yet he expected it. *Daily.* She might fascinate him, but he had no faith in her.

'What's wrong with pretty?' she repeated, her voice little more than a croak.

'You need to start taking risks with your art, Audrey. You need to experiment and free yourself from the usual conventions that hold you back.'

He's talking about artistic conventions.

He flicked negligent fingers at her sketchpad. 'Where is the movement? Where is the interest? What is the point?'

She stared at her sketch. She'd been so happy with it. Her brow furrowed. Pulling the pad closer she *really* stared at it. Swallowed. He was right, darn it.

'What were you thinking when you sketched that?'

'Just…how beautiful the scenery was. The beauty here overwhelms me. It's so different from home.' She moistened her lips. 'My sketch is pretty, but it's…sterile.'

'Because the beauty does not touch you here.' He pressed a hand to his chest. 'You need to find the courage to create the things that make you feel deeply. That is what will touch other people and draw them to your work.'

Her hands gripped each other tightly in her lap. 'What were you feeling when you sketched me?'

He hesitated. 'Anger.'

She flinched.

He shrugged, but he didn't apologise. 'I didn't say I was angry *with* you.'

No, but—

'Artists channel their emotions into forms and works that have no relation at all to the source of their emotion.'

She thought of the things she'd made in the aftermath of Jo's death, and nodded slowly.

'Will you sit for me?'

The question had her stiffening, though she realised belatedly she should've expected it. Maybe she should even feel flattered. But she didn't. Instead, she prickled and itched and burned and had to fight a scowl. What would he title the piece? *Before the Fall?*

'Will you sit for me?' she shot back instead. She could call hers *Pig-headed Male.*

His head rocked back.

And she crashed back with a thump, rushed back into speech. 'The answer is yes, of course I'll sit for you, Gabriel. It's not dependent on you sitting for me.'

He was doing so much for her, and she'd oblige

him in any way she could. If something in her had helped him overcome the block that had him in its grip for the past eight months, she'd be honoured to help him.

She gritted her teeth. *Honoured*, she repeated silently.

He leaned towards her. 'You would like me to sit for you?'

'I've never thought to take a person for my subject before.' She bit her lip. 'I've no idea if I could do it.'

'You have the skill.'

His quiet certainty had her straightening. 'You have a lot of faith in my abilities.'

'I do not understand why you don't have more faith in them yourself.'

Because, until now, she'd not had anyone recognise anything particularly wonderful about them. She'd never believed Nonna and Frankie when they'd told her how amazing her creations were. Oh, she knew they believed it, but they loved her. They were biased.

'How is it you've never pursued your art further? I do not understand. You tell me it is a passion of yours. Why, then, have you not attended art classes? And before you say you had neither the time nor opportunity to study art at university, there are night courses you could've taken. Hobby groups you could have joined. There your talent would've been recognised.'

His incredulity needled her. 'A person can have more than one passion.'

'What are these other passions of yours?'

'Family.'

He stared. With a muttered curse, he rubbed a hand over his face. 'I sometimes forget that not everyone is as caught up in their art as I am in mine. I apologise if I sounded uncompromising just then.'

She folded her arms. He was just like her father, caught up in his own world, uncaring and oblivious of anything—or anyone—else.

No, he's not.

Her heart started to thump. As soon as she'd been old enough, she'd looked after not just Johanna, but her father, too. Nonna had been getting on *and* was running a restaurant. And when Uncle Frank had died, Aunt Deidre had gone into such deep mourning, Audrey had refused to be an additional burden.

She hadn't minded looking after the house, though, and although her father had never said as much, she'd thought that he'd appreciated her efforts; she'd thought that she'd mattered to him. But she hadn't—at least, not as much as his own ambition. The way he'd just up and left for America, selling her childhood home from under her, proved that. Too late she'd realised she'd always given him more than he'd ever given her.

Was Gabriel like that? She moistened her lips. 'If you had to, would you give up your art for Lili?'

'Yes.' He watched her through hooded eyes. 'This is what you had to do for your family?' He let out a long breath. 'I'm sorry if you have been burdened with familial responsibilities and obligations that have prevented you from following your own dreams.'

She shot to her feet, her hands clenching so hard she started to shake. 'My family hasn't been *a burden*, Gabriel. Is that how you view Lili?'

His head rocked back. 'Of course not.'

'Then why would you say such a thing? I—'

Whirling away, she started to pace. She'd give up all of this—the chance to develop her art, Lake Como and all these riches—to have Johanna and Nonna back.

She swung around. 'You can't—'

Her words stuttered to a halt. He stood a hand's breadth away.

'I'm sorry.' Strong hands reached out to grip her shoulders, wrapping around them with a comforting warmth. It was the sincerity in his eyes that undid her, though. 'Audrey, I'm very sorry for upsetting you. I've blundered in with my blind judgements.' Those intriguing lips twisted. 'I'm always so sure I'm right. It is a failing of mine.'

The fight went out of her, just like that. She tried to smile and shrug at the same time but it emerged more like a hiccup. 'Forget about it.'

He led her back to the table, made her sit and then he went and made a pot of green tea and brought it out along with *chocolate biscuits*. She suddenly realised how ravenous she was.

'Please...' He gestured to the plate.

She needed no second bidding. Biting into a biscuit, she closed her eyes and let the sweetness coat her tongue. When she opened them again, she found him watching, but he quickly seized the teapot.

After pouring the tea, he pushed a cup towards her and then lifted his own and blew on it. 'I would like to hear about your family if you wish to talk of them. If Marguerite hasn't forbidden you from doing so.'

She felt a twang of sudden resentment at Marguerite. She had no right to ask her to keep Johanna a secret. Her gaze lowered to their sketchpads lying side by side. She recalled the threat that stretched through his sketch and hitched up her chin. Gabriel needed to know she had more strength than he'd given her credit for. She *wanted* him to know that.

'I had a twin.'

He froze.

'Her name was Johanna. Unfortunately, there were complications during the birth and she was starved of oxygen. She was diagnosed with cerebral palsy when she was fourteen months.'

He swore softly.

'It affected her movement and speech particularly. She could walk unassisted but it took a lot of effort so she mostly used a wheelchair. And while she could talk, it took her a long time to say what she wanted to. But she was whip smart and had a wicked sense of humour. She made you laugh at the most inopportune times.'

He smiled and she couldn't help but smile back. 'And,' she continued, 'took much delight in it, too, I might add. But she needed a lot of care.'

'And that care fell to you?'

'Nonna and Aunt Deidre helped out a lot. They basically raised us.'

'Where was your father all this time?'

'Playing the helpless male.' She rolled her eyes. 'I mean, we lived in the same house as him, which I can see now simply made more work for Nonna and my aunt. But they obviously thought it was the right thing to do—and it probably was—but single fatherhood was too much of a challenge for him, and he threw himself into his work instead.'

His lips thinned but he didn't say anything.

'We had part-time carers for Jo as well, but when I finished school I became her full-time carer. Not because anyone requested it of me, but because I wanted to. I loved her. She was my sister.'

Because of their father's preoccupation, she and Jo had become a team, had become each other's cheer squad. They'd shared everything—their hopes, dreams…secrets. She missed it more than she could say.

He nodded, no trace of judgement in his eyes. 'What happened to Johanna?'

'She died in a car accident four years ago. Just one of those freak things—a tyre blew out when they were on the freeway. The driver lost control and slammed into a truck.'

A strong tanned hand reached across and squeezed hers. 'I'm sorry.'

'Losing Johanna… That's when I realised how hard it is to love someone.'

'Because you sacrificed so much for her?'

'Because when I lost her, I felt I'd lost everything.'

That hand tightened about hers. 'Audrey, in some ways you did. You'd built your whole world around her.'

Of course he would think like that. She squeezed his hand back. 'I didn't lose everything, Gabriel. I still had Nonna and Aunt Deidre and Frankie, and Dad, even if he was rather detached. I still had the ability to work and earn a living. I had my embroideries.'

'And yet, even surrounded by all of those good things, a heart can break.'

And yet, broken hearts did mend.

She nodded at their joined hands, hers looking small and pale beside his. 'You're muscled and strong on the outside, Gabriel, while I look feeble in comparison. But don't let appearances fool you. I've had to be strong—for Johanna's sake and for my father's. And, yes, I know I'm out of my depth here in this brave new world I find myself in, but I will eventually find my feet. And I *will* be the director of my own destiny.'

Grey eyes met hers and he nodded. 'That's me put in my place, then.'

She bit her lip. 'I didn't mean it that way.'

'I know.'

To her relief he didn't look at all offended.

With one final squeeze, he reclaimed his hand and she tried to ignore the way her body protested the missing contact.

'Danae left when she discovered the issues Johanna would have to face in the future. I have no memory of her—Jo and I weren't even two years old yet.' She hitched up her chin. 'I'd never run away from the people I love. Especially when they needed me most.'

He remained silent.

'And I love Lili. I know I've only known her for a short time, but I love her. I plan to be there for her.' She shrugged, suddenly self-conscious. 'Just so you know.'

'I will sit for you, Audrey.'

She blinked at the sudden change of topic. His words and the pictures they evoked in her mind throwing her off balance. She leaned towards him. 'Really?'

'Would you like me to sit for you naked?' he said with a teasing glint in his eye.

Yes!

'No!' Heat flooded every atom of her being. Closing her eyes, she tried to shake the images from her mind. He chuckled and she knew she must be scarlet. Her eyes flew open and she pointed a finger at him. 'And I won't be posing for you naked, either.'

'What a shame.'

Her jaw dropped, but he merely threw his head back and laughed. 'Johanna would've enjoyed the joke, I'm sure.'

She snorted then, too. Seizing another chocolate biscuit, she held the plate out to him. 'Have a biscuit and stop teasing me.'

But he didn't. He'd stilled. *'That's* why you asked me about charities and how to become a patron. You want to set something up in Johanna's name.'

'Maybe.' She wished her voice didn't sound so suddenly small or defensive.

He stood and stalked to the edge of the clearing. When he turned back, he widened his stance. 'Marguerite has banned you from talking about Johanna, hasn't she?'

She didn't want to answer, but he clearly read the answer in her face. Giving a harsh laugh, he shook his head. 'I should've realised sooner. She wouldn't want the wider world knowing she'd had a granddaughter who was anything other than physically perfect. Heaven forbid anyone suspect something so shocking.'

'No,' she croaked. 'I'm sure you're wrong. I think she finds it painful she never met her.'

A sceptical look crossed his face and he folded his arms. 'How do you think you're going to get Marguerite's approval for a foundation in Johanna's name? How do you think you're going to reconcile her to you talking freely about Johanna *publicly*?'

That, of course, was the question. Because as things currently stood, Marguerite couldn't tolerate so much as the mention of Johanna's name. But it'd get better. She swallowed. It *would* get better. *If wishes were fishes...*

She pushed that thought away. Marguerite *had* to reconcile herself to Audrey's talking about Johanna publicly because nobody, not even the Funaros, would have her turning her back on her sister. Even if it meant they'd disown her. 'She just needs time.'

He gave a disbelieving laugh.

Pain pounded behind her eyes. 'I'm going to talk to her about it...soon. And then you'll see.'

Those infuriating brows rose.

'You'll be eating your words before you know it.'

CHAPTER EIGHT

'IS CONVERSATION BANNED while I sit?'

Gabriel was midstretch when Audrey asked her question. If she'd asked him five minutes earlier, he'd have probably not even heard her. He hadn't been this intensely captured by a work in…

He couldn't remember.

Thankfully, his creative drought was at an end. He felt alive, invigorated, as if all of his body was breathing again.

Despite that, his instinct was to answer in the negative and demand silence as he was working. But she'd agreed to sit for him without a murmur of complaint. It'd be churlish of him to refuse.

'We can talk if you like…as long as you don't move too much.'

He had her sitting on a mound of cushions on the floor—a make-believe rock—with her face turned towards the wall of glass, side on to him. She held her sketchpad and a pencil.

She chuckled. 'You didn't complain a little while ago when I stretched out a cramp in my calf. You were clearly immersed in your drawing.'

He glanced at the clock and swore. '*Dio*, Audrey, it has been two hours! Why didn't you say something? You can get up and move if you wish.'

'I'm fine. You have me for another half an hour and then I'm done, so you might as well make the most of it.'

He picked up his pencil again. He would refine what he could in the next thirty minutes. 'In light of your patience, I'll even start a conversation.'

Those mobile lips curved upwards and he wondered how he could capture their compelling combination of softness and strength. And what would be the better material to use to capture them—steel or wood?

Doing his best to ignore the heat prickling through his veins and the persistent ache of his groin, he dragged his mind to the promised conversation. 'Why, when I asked you to wear your oldest, most comfortable jeans when you were sitting for me, did you not just wear them for the whole day? Why did you bring them to get changed into?'

She started to shrug, but stopped as if remembering she was supposed to be still. 'Because I didn't want Marguerite to see me in them.'

He scowled. 'Why would it matter if she did?'

She huffed out a laugh. 'Are you scowling, Gabriel?'

He cleared his face. 'Absolutely not.'

'Because she doesn't like them, and I don't wish to upset her.'

'You don't have to live your whole life to please her. Why even consider doing such a thing?'

'You ask the wrong question.' She turned her head a couple of inches to meet his gaze and the expression in her spice-coloured eyes had his pulse picking up speed. 'Ask yourself *why* these jeans bother her so much.'

That was simple. 'Because they do not fit the sleek, sophisticated image she would wish for a granddaughter of the Funaro family.' As far as Marguerite was concerned, the image the Funaros presented had to be perfect.

'You're wrong.' She turned to stare back out at the window, but where before the lines of her body had been passive, they were now firm—that pointed chin squared and those eyes narrowed. 'These jeans remind her that I grew up in a world far removed from hers. They remind her of all the years we didn't know each other and can't get back. The sight of my old, shabby jeans makes her grieve, because she wasn't there to help out financially or to offer any kind of emotional support when I was growing up.'

Her words made something in his chest cramp. 'You imbue her with feelings she doesn't have.'

'While you seem determined to believe she has no feelings at all.'

He rolled his shoulders. That wasn't true. Was it?

'Tell me about Serafina.'

'No!' The word shot out of him with the violence of a summer storm, and he found himself breathing hard. The request had taken him by surprise, but it shouldn't have.

Audrey flinched, but a moment later resumed the pose. 'Why not?'

'I do not talk about Fina.'

Her entire body drooped as she let out a breath. 'Nobody does. You must all miss her very much.'

His fingers tightened about his pencil. She had no idea. And he had no intention of enlightening her.

'She was so young. And so beautiful.'

Oh, yes, Fina had been very beautiful. On the outside.

'Lili is going to want to know about her, you know. Eventually, she'll start asking more demanding questions, and she won't be put off with one-word answers. She'll expect more from you.'

He knew that. But it wouldn't be for several years yet. He had time to work out what he would say. And maybe time will have softened him, and he'd be able to utter the lies without giving himself away. He scowled. 'Why are you so interested in Fina anyway?'

She turned fully around to face him. 'She was my *sister*. How would you feel if you suddenly discovered a sibling you never knew you'd had? Wouldn't you want to know all about him or her?'

'Assume the pose, please.' She did, but it didn't ease the burning in his soul. Her words had found their mark, but they didn't make him any more eager to talk about Serafina. Yes, he understood her curiosity, but if she'd ever met Fina, she'd have been disappointed in the other woman.

Bitterly.

Just as he had been.

'Fine, then tell me about Vittoria, Livia and Adriana.'

Her cousins? 'Why?'

'Because I'm having lunch with them tomorrow.'

And so it begins...

This family would engulf her, take her over and re-create her into their own image. They'd destroy her. He threw his pencil down. 'We're done here for the moment.'

She glanced around, registered the expression on his face and nodded. But as she started to rise, she winced and grabbed her calf. He immediately moved to assist her, his hand reaching down to hers. Her fingers tightened in his and she gasped and hopped. 'Gah, cramp! I'm not used to sitting so still for so long.'

As a nurse's aide, she must spend long days on her feet. He should've taken that into account and ensured she had regular stretching breaks.

Kneeling down, he brushed her hands aside, working his fingers on the calf muscle that had tightened beneath the soft denim of her jeans. She gasped, groaned and half hopped. 'Lean against my shoulder,' he ordered.

A hand immediately landed on his shoulder, and the soft weight of her and the feel of her warm flesh beneath the thin, butter-soft denim made him aware of her in a way he'd been trying to avoid all morning. Her scent swamped him, invading his lungs and moving with a slow surety to his blood, his limbs growing languid. As the tightness in her calf gave way beneath his hand, his fingers, too, became more leisurely—exploring, caressing, wanting to learn the shape of her.

He suddenly found his hands empty.

'It's all good now, thanks,' she choked out.

Rising, he found her eyes wide and dark colour staining her cheeks.

'Where did you learn to massage like that? It's very effective. I'm dying for a coffee. You?'

She was babbling and he knew why—because she felt the pull between them, too. And because of Marguerite, she was determined to ignore it.

And because of you.

Dragging a hand down his face, he nodded. He'd told her not to fall in love with him or to think of him in any kind of romantic way. Just because Marguerite was of the same mind didn't mean he had to change his.

Dio! He knew he was bitter, but what kind of man would it make him if he seduced Audrey simply to disoblige Marguerite? He was not in the habit of breaking hearts and destroying people. He left that to the likes of the Funaros.

Audrey had moved to the kitchenette and he dragged in a breath and tried to steady himself.

'I used to play football when I was younger. Not professionally. I wasn't that good. But I played for years in a local league. Cramps were common.'

When she finally turned back, her colour was normal again. Handing him a coffee, she took a turn about the studio, studying the various pieces he'd started and abandoned. 'So, Vittoria, Livia and Adriana?'

His nose curled.

'It seems to me you don't like to talk about any of the Funaros.'

'Esattamente,' he muttered. *Exactly.*

'But nor do you want me letting Lili down. You want me to be a regular fixture in her life.' She turned and pinned him with those eyes. 'So help me fit in here, Gabriel. Explain the undercurrents and all the things I'm in ignorance of.'

A dark anger pierced him. This woman deserved so much more. 'How can family mean so much to you when your own parents were the antithesis of what family stood for?' How could she still have so much faith in family?

'My parents got it wrong. For heaven's sake, why would I emulate them? Why would I make the same mistakes they did?' She pointed a finger at him. 'It was my nonna who got it right. *That's* who I want to emulate.'

With the Funaros? Was she mad?

Those dark eyes narrowed and sparks flashed in their depths as if she could read his thoughts in his face. 'Nonna gave me so much. She taught me that there's strength in a family, not to mention a sense of belonging and love. She *proved* that to me. And I'm going to do everything in my power to create that with my family here in Italy. I'll continue the legacy she gave me.'

He opened his mouth.

'And just because I wasn't enough for my father or my mother, doesn't mean I won't be enough for Marguerite or the rest of the Funaros.'

He wanted to swear.

'And just because *you* don't value family, doesn't mean the rest of us feel the same way!'

He valued family!

'And just because the Funaros aren't enough for you, doesn't mean they're not enough for me!'

He gaped at her.

'Family matters *so much*. I'd hate to think what would've happened to Jo if it weren't for Nonna and Aunt Deidre.'

Or Audrey, he added silently.

'If she'd been alone in the world...' She shuddered. 'It doesn't bear thinking about. And *I* don't want to be alone in the world, either. What if something happened to me? Who could I turn to?'

His hands clenched at the thought.

'I know you're besotted with this whole "I'm a lone wolf and untouchable" thing you've got going on.'

'My...*what*?'

'But there's a reason solitary confinement is a punishment. People weren't meant to be isolated and alone. And just because family politics are tiresome and some family members can be annoying, doesn't mean one shouldn't make the best of what they've got.'

'Have you not heard the proverb that you can't make a silk purse from a sow's ear?' he ground out.

She clenched her hands so hard she shook. 'Vittoria, Livia and Adriana?'

After dragging in a breath, he let it out slowly. He couldn't force Audrey to see what she didn't want to see. Eventually, he nodded. 'Vittoria went into business with a friend—fashion, I think… Something to do with earrings if I'm not mistaken. Anyway, she plugged a great deal of money into it, but it was a failure. Marguerite refused to bankroll her any further.'

She bit her lip. He did his best to not notice how it deepened the colour and plumped it—as if she'd just been kissed. Her colour was still high from their somewhat heated exchange and… He swallowed. Audrey would look sublime mussed up after a bout of vigorous lovemaking.

Dio! Stop imagining such things.

'Livia was at the centre of a sex scandal. An ex-boyfriend leaked a piece of naked footage he'd taken of her on his phone.'

Her eyes widened. 'That's appalling.'

'Welcome to the world of the Funaros.'

She rolled her eyes. 'And Adriana?'

'Has recently returned from drug rehab.'

Her shoulders slumped. 'Okay, so that's…a lot.'

'They each have a big black mark against their name as far as Marguerite is concerned.'

'And are all desperate to make amends.'

It was true that all of them would like to be in Marguerite's good books.

'And what about some of the older family members—my mother's contemporaries—like Caterina, Anna, Nicolo and Davide? There's going to be a dinner later in the week.'

They were the children of Marguerite's siblings. He filled her in on some of the family politics.

She listened in silence. When he was done, she pointed to one of his sculptures. 'Next time I sit for you, would I be able to look at that?'

He frowned. 'Why?'

'I don't know, but there's something about it…' She fixed him with a frown. 'Surely, it's an easy enough question—yes or no?'

'*Si*, if you wish it.'

Her shoulders and jaw relaxed. 'Thank you.'

Something inside him unhitched then, too, but for the life of him he couldn't explain what it was.

'How did your lunch with Vittoria, Livia and Adriana go?' Gabriel asked the following Monday when she was once again sitting for him.

He'd arranged the sculpture on a low table in front of her. Her attention had been fixed on it for the past hour, and it was her attitude of concentration that had caught his fancy today. He glanced down at his sketch and nodded, satisfied.

'Okay, I think. I liked them.'

That surprised him.

'And the dinner with Caterina, Anna, Nicolo and Davide?'

'Okay, too, I think.'

The brevity of her answers needled him. 'Was Marguerite at the dinner?'

Her dark hair fanned about her face when she shook her head. 'She had other plans.'

He froze. 'Marguerite left you to face the slathering horde alone?'

'I told her I was more than capable of going alone. And they're not a slathering horde.' She bit her lip. 'Though they're all a bit reserved.'

By reserved, he bet she meant rude, impenetrable and unwelcoming.

She gestured at his sketchpad. 'Are we done?' At his nod, she rose and shook out her arms and legs. 'They're not exactly a happy bunch, are they?'

'You know you could just walk away from them.' He hated the thought of her expending time and energy on people who didn't have her best interests at heart. 'You don't owe these people anything.'

She turned her back on him. 'We've had this conversation before. That's *not* what family does. And as I already know you don't want me walking away from Lili, why should I walk away from anyone else?'

She had a point even if he didn't want to admit it.

She turned. 'I'm also including you in my *not a happy bunch* comment.'

He stiffened. 'Not happy? *Me?* I'm happy!'

'Shout a little louder. I'm sure that'll convince me.'

He scowled. When he wasn't stuck at Lake Como on the Funaro estate, he was happy.

And when he didn't have a creative block.

And when he didn't have to think about Fina or the legacy she'd left their daughter.

'Gabriel, when was the last time you played football?'

He blinked to find her staring at him with her head cocked to one side. 'I... A long time.'

'Maybe you ought to take it back up again.'

'Why?'

One shoulder lifted in an elegantly eloquent shrug. 'Why not? Exercise is good for the soul as well as the body. Maybe you've got into a rut and that's why you've been having trouble with your sculptures. Maybe you need to try new things, do different things... Have some fun.'

She might have a point, and if he could've focused on it, he might have pursued it further, but… He pointed a shaking finger at her shoulder. 'Have you been having *deportment* lessons?'

She jumped up and down on the spot, clapping her hands. 'You can tell?'

It was *awful*!

'You've no idea how wonderful it is to have your body say exactly what you want it to, to *behave* exactly as you want it to.'

She… It—

'No, scrap that.' Her soft laugh slammed into him. 'You're a master at silent communication. You know *exactly* how empowering it is.'

He had absolutely no comeback for that.

CHAPTER NINE

AUDREY CLOSED THE villa's front door as quietly as she could. Leaning against the door to catch her breath, she slipped off her high heels. What a night.

She was too keyed up for bed, even though it was the wee small hours of the morning. And she was starving. An image of the cake she'd made earlier in the day rose in her mind but before she could turn in the direction of the kitchen, footsteps sounded on the stairs.

She immediately straightened—slouching was bad, or so her deportment teacher informed her—but relaxed again when her gaze collided with the piercing grey of Gabriel's. Somewhere deep inside a tic started up.

'Do you know what time it is?' he hissed when he reached the bottom stair.

She gurgled back a laugh, pitying future teenage Lili. 'Yes, I do.' She folded her arms. 'What do you mean by staying out so late, Gabriel?'

His mouth opened but no words came out.

She took pity on him. 'Hungry?'

Not waiting for an answer, she made for the kitchen, going to the hidden spot on the other side of the island where Anna the cook had secreted the cake. Lifting it up, she raised an eyebrow in question.

'You're having a midnight feast?'

She giggled. 'Technically, I think you'll find it's a 2 a.m. feast.'

Dark brows lowered. 'Are you drunk?'

She set the cake on the bench between them. 'A little tipsy, perhaps, but not rolling drunk. You get the milk while I cut the cake.'

His eyes practically started from their sockets. 'Milk?'

'Yes, it comes in cartons and is usually kept on the top shelf of the refrigerator, which is that huge stainless-steel monolith over there and—'

'Yes, yes, thank you.' Without another word he grabbed two glasses and the carton of milk and then hesitated. 'Do you want it heated?'

She shuddered. 'Hot milk is disgusting. Cold milk is perfection.'

With lips twitching, he set a glass in front of her and filled it to the brim. 'Do you know how many calories are in this?' He gestured at their feast.

'If that's the stance you mean to take with Lili as she's growing up, I'm afraid we're going to butt heads.'

'I…no. But Marguerite would have a fit if she could see you now.'

That made her laugh. 'Marguerite told me slim women held all the power, but I pooh-poohed that idea. I told her *healthy* women held all the power. I said, *It's the twenty-twenties, Grandmother, not the nineteen-sixties, when Twiggy was all the rage.* She found the idea…not without merit.'

He stared.

Pulling one of the plates towards her, she forked a generous mouthful of sponge into her mouth, relishing the sweet softness of cake, the hint of raspberry jam and fresh cream. 'Try it,' she ordered when he remained rooted to the spot. 'It's my signature cake.'

'*You* made this?'

'Why so surprised?'

'Everything you do surprises me,' he muttered. 'You're nothing like any of us expected.'

She was starting to think that could be a good thing.

Ignoring his fork, he lifted the cake in his fingers. A firm mouth and strong white teeth bit into it. She held her breath as he blinked, his eyes widening…and then he took another gigantic bite and swore softly in a way that sounded like a caress. 'You are a witch.'

'Why are your eyes grey? I like them, but the colour is unusual.'

'Are you sure you're not drunk?'

'Pretty sure. It's a 2 a.m. thing, I think.' She ate more cake and sipped her milk. 'People have a tendency to say things they wouldn't normally say in the wee small hours.'

'Where were you tonight?'

'Where were you?'

'Having dinner with a prospective client.'

And he'd checked on Lili before going back to his cottage. Because of course he had.

'I was out dancing with the girls.'

'The girls?'

'Tori, Livy and Ana.'

He leaned towards her. 'Who?'

'Vittoria, Livia and Adriana.'

'You've given them pet names?'

'Nicknames are a big thing in Australia—a sign of affection.' When he didn't say anything, she added, 'If you lived in Australia, you'd be called Gabe. But I prefer Gabriel. It suits you.'

'And what is your name shortened to?'

'Aud, sometimes, but that's not very pretty.'

'No, I prefer Audrey.'

They finished their cake and milk.

'Did you enjoy the dancing?'

She suppressed a yawn as she rinsed their plates and glasses before popping them in the dishwasher. 'Very much. Due to various things over the years, there hasn't been too much dancing in my life. Not that I'm complaining. But tonight was a real treat. I danced so hard I earned my cake.'

'And is that all you did?'

'Of course not. We chatted—girl talk, you know—and drank French champagne, which is *truly* delicious.' She winced. 'Though, it's wickedly expensive.' Apparently, she had the money to indulge such treats these days, but it was still hard not to count pennies when she'd been doing so all her life.

'Anything else?'

He'd gone all stiff and disapproving, and she suddenly realised what he was asking. He wanted to know if she'd indulged in any flirtations. 'That's really none of your business, Gabriel.' Normally, she was conciliatory, but he made her want to throw things with his casually negative judgements. 'Just because I go out dancing and enjoy a couple of drinks with the girls doesn't make me a bad person. It doesn't mean I'm about to self-destruct. And neither does meeting a man who might take my fancy and exploring that further. So you can take your nasty mind and its vile conclusions and shove them where the sun doesn't shine.'

His head rocked back. He opened his mouth, but she shook her head. 'You're acting like a dog in the manger. And I don't get it.' She leaned in close and his swift intake of breath speared into the centre of her, the chill in his eyes replaced with a heart-stopping heat...and that heat started to inch through her, too. She snapped back before she fell into them and did something totally *stupid*.

'It wouldn't matter if I were the most perfect woman in the world.' She said it for her own benefit as much as his. 'The fact that I'm a member of the Funaro family is a black mark I can never overcome.' He wouldn't fall in love with her on principle—because it would mean having to forgive the Funaros and he had no intention of doing that. 'In your eyes I will always be tainted by association.'

He stiffened. 'I...'

She huffed out a laugh. 'You can't even offer me friendship. I mean, if you were even so much as friends with me the world would come tumbling down, right?'

He blinked.

'So here's the thing, Gabriel. You don't get to tell me who I can and cannot date, any more than Marguerite can.'

He started to say something but she cut him off.

'Don't say a word. I repeat... It's. None. Of. Your. Business.'

With that she turned and walked away.

Audrey eased back to stare at her handiwork, the light outside that enormous window flooding the studio and haloing the piece she'd been working on. She'd created a glittering web of golds and blue, but threaded beneath it here and there were strands of black and grey—the exact same grey as Gabriel's eyes.

She glanced around, but he was working on something and had his back to her—as if deliberately ignoring her. It had been a week since that incident in the kitchen, and while he'd apologised

to her the next day, the memory of it still somehow throbbed between them.

It was there when she sat for him.

It was there when he explained some detail of
his methodology.

It was there when they explored the work of
other fibre artists.

And it was there in his eyes whenever she spent
time with Lili.

Shaking the thought off, she focused on the
web and backdrop she'd created and then glanced
across at the sculpture she'd studied so thoroughly
while sitting for him. It was a clay model of something he'd probably hoped to eventually make on
a far greater scale from recycled metal and tim-
ber. At the moment it wasn't much more than a
fluid shape half a metre tall, but nevertheless, the
outline suggested to her a figure wrestling with…
well, itself, she supposed.

The web she'd made was supported on seven
sticks she'd sourced from fallen branches outside,
and she wanted to place it over the sculpture, en-
gulfing it. She'd taken measurements, had envisaged it in place…

She now needed to see it all as one piece before she decided how she ought to continue with
the backdrop, which was the piece of linen from
which all the threads emanated. Glancing across at
Gabriel, she bit her lip. If she was quiet, she could
tiptoe over to the sculpture, set the frame in place,

assess the effect and then tiptoe the frame back to her workbench. If she was quick and careful, Gabriel would be none the wiser.

She couldn't explain why she didn't want to share this with him yet. It's just…she wanted it perfect before he gave her feedback. And she didn't want to risk either his scorn or indignation that she'd improvised from a work of his. Maybe he'd think she was taking advantage of him.

She grimaced. Maybe he'd be right.

In the next moment she thrust out her chin. He'd told her to experiment. That was what she was doing.

Glancing across again and assuring herself that Gabriel was utterly immersed in whatever he was working on, she picked up her intricate web and moved silently across to the sculpture on its low table and set her frame in place.

After easing back a couple of steps, she crouched down to view it. Her pulse suddenly quickened. She'd never created anything like this before—but the moment she'd conceived it, it had consumed her.

Rubbing her nape, she nodded. She was definitely on the right track. Straightening, she went to remove the frame, when a commanding voice behind her bellowed, 'Do not touch it!'

She froze. *Damn.* She should've waited until he'd gone outside for a walk or a coffee.

Though his footsteps were silent, she could feel

him moving closer. He stopped just behind her. She could feel the heat that flowed from him and the invigorating sting of his scent. Combined, they made her feel both confused and alive. Like so much about this man, her reaction made no sense.

She did what she could to channel Marguerite's unflappable calm—but inside butterflies the size of seagulls squawked and divebombed. Pressing her hands to her waist, she kept her gaze firmly fixed on the piece before them. She would *not* be the first to speak.

In fact, she shifted her weight and continued what she'd been doing in the first place—assessing the piece and deciding what else she could do to improve it. She'd take her time. Gabriel kept telling her she was an artist. Fine! She'd act like one, then.

Making a circuit around the piece, she halted at the backdrop that she was still in the process of embroidering. From the statue side the threads shot out to the rest of the frame, but on this side she was trying to create an abstract pattern.

'What are you thinking?'

He spoke from beside her, and she pointed. 'I need to remove the black.'

'And replace it with…?'

'Pink.' She frowned. Pink hadn't been part of the colour palette she'd used, but she instinctively knew it would work. It would create a contrast—not lightening the piece like gold or blue would, but softening it. 'And, actually, I'll keep a thread of black here and here.'

'Why?'

'Because it's what's true to the piece. It will make it more…human.'

They continued their circuit until they stood in front of it once again.

'What are you titling it?' When she didn't immediately answer he offered, *'Tangled Web?'*

She shook her head. There was nothing tangled about her web. It was quite deliberate. *'Ties That Bind,'* she decided.

'Audrey.'

She finally turned and met his gaze. Grey eyes raked hers and firm lips lifted. 'Excellent.'

'What?' She frowned. The piece? Her experimentation? Or…?

'You do not care what I think of this piece. It is something of which you are happy to take complete ownership. It is something of which you are proud.'

His words made her blink. 'I am proud of it,' she agreed. 'But it's not entirely true that I don't care what you think.'

'But if I told you this was rubbish?'

She shrugged. 'I'd continue to work on it.' *She'd* still like it.

'*Si*, this is what I mean.' He considered the piece again. 'But in this instance, we're in agreement. What you have done here, it is extraordinary.'

He really thought so?

'I can see how beautifully you've incorporated what you learned from our studies of both Marley and Sinestra.'

She couldn't prevent her hands from going to her hips. 'Then why haven't you called it derivative?' Which is what he'd called a piece she'd been working on earlier in the week.

'Because here you have employed the techniques in your own unique fashion.' That gaze settled on her, a crease deepening his brow. 'If my derivative comment stung, you perhaps need to grow a thicker skin.'

'And maybe you need to recognise that I work differently than you. You see something new and immediately want to experiment with it. I see something new and want to practise the technique to know that I can master it before I begin experimenting.'

He eased away a fraction farther to survey her more critically. Eventually, he nodded. 'There is a reason I am an artist and not a teacher.'

His words immediately had guilt crashing down on her. 'You're an excellent teacher, Gabriel. I shouldn't have inferred otherwise. I've learned an enormous amount from you and I'm very grateful.'

He merely shrugged. 'You are a consummate recycler, too, because I had every intention of throwing that sculpture away. Now instead, I can gift it to you.'

She gaped at him. 'You can't do that!'

He thrust out his chin at a haughty angle. 'I can do what I wish with my own work. Would you prefer that I throw it in the bin for you to retrieve later?'

'Of course not. I—'

'Then accept this gift in the spirit it was given—a gift from one artist to another. You had a vision for the sculpture where I did not. You've *earned* the sculpture.'

She stared at him, blinking.

'Simply say thank you and accept the gift.'

Drawing in a breath, she nodded. 'Thank you.' She knew precisely how extraordinary such a gift was.

Gabriel could sense how much Audrey wanted to get back to work, but he couldn't let the piece go just yet. Even unfinished, it captured the attention and held it hostage. 'This needs to be shown.'

'I beg your pardon.'

Her incredulity had him smiling. Maybe once she saw other people's reactions to her work, she would finally start to believe in herself. Before the summer was over, they might have enough of her work assembled to hold an exhibition.

'How many exhibitions have you been to since arriving in Italy?'

'Only a couple. I saw one in Rome before com-

ing to Lake Como, and then another in Como.
Though I have spent a lot of time at the art gallery.'

'Would you like to attend the new exhibition
at the Galleria Pensiero with me in a fortnight?'

She started to dance on the spot. 'Are you serious? I'd give my eyeteeth to go to an opening
night like that one.'

He shook his head, but he suspected his eyes
might be dancing, too. 'Then you need to tell Marguerite's secretary and she will ensure you get all
such future invitations.'

Her mouth dropped open. 'Just like that?'

He couldn't explain why, but she made him
want to laugh; she made him feel young again.
Even now she had no idea what doors her name
and fortune could open for her. 'Just like that.'

'Wow.'

'But in this instance, you can come as my guest,
yes? There are several people from the art world
I would like you to meet.'

'Are you sure it's no bother?'

'Of course it isn't. It will be an interesting night
and should be fun to compare opinions on the
different pieces. Consider it part of your ongoing
education.'

'Then thank you. I'd like that very much.'

'It's finally finished.'

Audrey had continued working on *Ties That
Bind* for the rest of the week and Gabriel set

down his tools now and moved across to where she stood.

Every time she'd left the room during the past week, he'd found himself drawn across to it. Something in it ruffled his soul, made him feel too much. He could count on the fingers of one hand the artworks that had such an impact on him.

The finished piece was shocking. And beautiful. The longer he stared at it, the more his heart ached.

'What's wrong?'

The quiet question throbbed between them.

'Gabriel?'

His name on her lips broke the spell and had him slamming back. He swallowed and gestured. 'It is powerful.'

She sucked her bottom lip into her mouth; her forehead creased. 'I can hardly believe I created such a thing.'

He knew what she meant. He sometimes felt like that when he finished an installation. Somewhere between vision and execution, a work could take on a life of its own.

'Is that how you see yourself?' he suddenly burst out. 'Trapped behind a beautiful web and unable to break free?' Because while there was no denying the beauty of the web, it still held the figure fast inside.

Her brow pleated.

'I mean, you have made the figure strong. Or

at least you have given the sculpture an appearance of strength.' But that didn't change the fact that the figure was trapped.

She stared at the piece. 'Is that how you see it?'

Did she not?

Shaking her head, she met his gaze. 'That's not me, Gabriel.'

Her face confirmed the truth of her words. He couldn't explain why, but something inside him unclenched and he was able to breathe again. He did not want her feeling trapped like that. This woman deserved to be free.

Gabriel was aware of the glances he and Audrey drew as they entered the Galleria Pensiero, but he ignored them. The gallery was built on classic lines, and the inside foyer was a soaring auditorium of Italian marble and sparkling chandeliers, the light glinting off crystal glasses balanced on elegant trays circulated about the room by stylish waitstaff.

At his side Audrey gave a dreamy sigh, and for once he agreed with her. With practised ease, he seized two champagne flutes from a passing tray and handed her one. Smiling her thanks, she touched her glass to his before taking a sip, her lids fluttering in appreciation.

In that moment he knew she would never take French champagne for granted; that she would always acknowledge the wonder of it with every sip. The knowledge lifted something inside him. Fina had knocked the stuff back like there was no tomorrow. She hadn't cared whether it was French champagne, vodka, or a nice Brunello. It had all been one and the same to her.

Maybe, just maybe, Audrey would be able to avoid the same fate as her mother and sister. For a moment he allowed himself to hope. He would do whatever he could to make sure she had all the props and supports she needed; that she had something to fall back on. Something other than drugs, alcohol and sex. And then Lili would have at least one female relative she could take as a role model.

'Thank you so much for bringing me tonight, Gabriel.'

'You have already thanked me three times. This thanks is not necessary.' He gestured for them to move towards the works on display. 'It is my responsibility as your mentor to ensure you receive ample opportunities for development, yes?'

She glanced across, a frown in her eyes. 'And what about when we are no longer mentor and mentee?'

'We will still be colleagues.' They could continue to discuss art and the projects they were working on. She would still be Lili's aunt.

'Not friends?'

When he didn't answer immediately, the light in her eyes dimmed and it left him feeling like a heel.

He hated having put that expression in her eyes. But could he and this woman ever be friends?

She sipped her champagne. 'That's clearly a *no*, then.'

What if they became friends and then she followed in Danae and Fina's footsteps, after all? Where would that leave him and Lili? He swallowed, his collar drawing tight about his throat. 'I do not give my friendship quickly,' he finally said. 'I am not one of these people who needs a lot of friends. But the ones I have I take very good care of.'

'That's good to know.' But the happy sparkle in her eyes didn't return.

'I am not saying we will not be friends.'

She nodded, but didn't look at him, pointed instead at the painting they surveyed. 'That's an interesting colour combination.'

They were both silent as they assessed the painting before moving along to the next one.

'In the meantime—' she swung back, her attempt at restraint clearly failing '—you'll just keep fatalistically waiting for the worst to happen and miss out on all the good things friendships—and family—can give you?'

He choked on his wine. Was she inferring…? 'The Funaros are *not* my family.' He kept his voice low but the words shot from him like paint splatter.

'Of course they are. You married into them, didn't you? They're Lili's family.'

'But—'

'Sure, you can keep your distance and be all grumpy and broody and disapproving. But it doesn't change the facts.'

You bet your life he'd keep his distance, but he couldn't prevent a thread of curiosity from rising through him then, too. 'How, I would like to know, do you think I could—' he searched for an appropriate word '—*integrate* myself into the family?'

'By getting to know them better… Socialising and mixing with them. Like, for example, attending the surprise seventy-fifth birthday party I'm throwing for Marguerite.'

She was doing *what*? Marguerite would *hate* a surprise party.

'I don't like this piece.' She scrunched up her face at the canvas in front of them. 'Odd, as I can see the expertise, the superiority of the artist's technique.'

He found himself in accord, but he didn't say that out loud. It was strange how attuned they could be about art, and yet how out of step they were when it came to family.

'It would mean a lot to Lili.'

He knew that, but… Huffing out an exasperated breath, he glared at her. 'You are not easy company.'

'Not true! I'm very easy company when I sit for you.'

Then she thankfully seemed content with her

own thoughts and kept them to herself, instead of giving voice to them and ruffling his mood.

'Ah.' He looked up. 'I just spotted Marco. I would like to introduce you to him. He is an agent and I suspect he would be very interested in what you are doing with your fibre art.'

She stared up at him with deer-in-the-headlights eyes, her throat bobbing as she swallowed.

'No.' He pointed a commanding finger at her. 'You are not going to be nervous or self-effacing. You are going to own the fact that you are an artist and that the work you are doing is unique and powerful and needs to find a greater audience.'

'Oh, but—'

'No buts! You have talent. You will project confidence and conviction in your work.'

The glass in her hand wobbled.

'Close your eyes.'

She did as he said. Staring into that beautiful face with the hair gathered up high on her head and dark ringlets falling down around her neck, a deep hunger surged through him. He ground his teeth against it. 'Picture in your mind your *Ties That Bind* piece. Recall how you feel about it—the pride you have in it and the wonder—revel in the knowledge that you created it.'

She swallowed. The glass in her hand steadied and she opened her eyes. 'Okay, you're right. I have work I'm proud of. I'll do my best not to embarrass you.'

Her words softened something at the centre of him. 'I know you won't. Even if you did, I wouldn't care. But I do not wish you to do yourself a disservice. This is all.'

Taking her arm, he manoeuvred her towards Marco. 'You once asked me about the colour of my eyes.'

She swung to him. 'I did! You never did tell me where they came from.'

'From my mother. She was half Irish.'

She stared. 'Have you been to Ireland?'

'Si.'

'Do you have family there?'

What was it about this woman and family? 'A couple of distant cousins.'

'How lovely. Tell me. Is Ireland as green as everyone says?'

He nodded. 'I'm sure you would find it most inspiring. Marco!' He hailed the agent. 'It is good to see you.'

He made the introductions, and with a few choice words didn't just pique the agent's interest in Audrey's work, but had him covetous to be the first agent to see it.

'Is this piece really as extraordinary as you say?' Marco demanded, handing Audrey his card.

'It's one of the most powerful artworks I have ever seen.'

Marco took Audrey's hand. 'You must contact

me soon, yes? I will come view your work and then—'

'Excuse us. I just spotted someone I'd like Audrey to meet.' Gabriel smoothly detached Audrey from the other man's grip and whisked her off to introduce her to a rival agent. Marco would be the perfect agent for Audrey, but he'd appreciate her all the more if he had to fight for her.

'Oh, my God! Oh, my God!' Audrey chanted under her breath for his ears only.

'Smile. Chin up. Confident, remember?'

She gurgled back a laugh. 'Would it appal you to realise how much like Marguerite you just sounded then?'

He tried to feel affronted, but couldn't manage it. He satisfied himself with a flippant, 'Do not spoil the evening.'

Her laugh made him grin.

CHAPTER TEN

'AT BREAKFAST THIS MORNING Lili was talking about this party you're planning for Marguerite.'

Audrey halted midstretch, glancing up from the piece she was currently working on—a traditional embroidery on a piece of square linen the colour of midnight—and realised Gabriel's hammering and welding had been nonexistent for the past twenty minutes. Had he been waiting for her, not wanting to break her concentration?

Shaking herself, she completed her stretch. 'She's very excited about it. Coffee?' She started towards the kitchenette. 'Of course, when you're four, parties *are* very exciting.'

'I will make the coffee if you will cut whatever sweet wickedness you brought with you today.'

She'd cut the chocolate brownies before they'd left the villa—leaving instructions with Maria that both Lili and Marguerite had one for their morning coffee as well—but she dished them out now onto the plain white plates he kept in the cupboard.

As had become their habit, they took their mid-morning coffee outside to the wooden table, sitting on the same bench so as to face the lake and drink in the view. Not so closely, though, that shoulders or thighs brushed. She could feel the heat that emanated from him, though, as warm against her left side as the sun overhead.

'Audrey, do you have much experience with children?'

'A couple of my girlfriends have children, and I enjoy their company on the odd occasion I get the chance. Why?'

A frown creased his brow and her heart plummeted. 'Have I done something wrong with Lili?' Her hands clenched. She'd never knowingly do anything to hurt her delightful little niece.

'That is not what I meant. It is just...'

He turned to face her more fully, his knee bumping hers, sending a rush of awareness streaking through her. She tried to look unmoved, but heat crept into her cheeks, no doubt turning them pink. She hoped he misread it as her horror of doing something that would harm Lili.

He shuffled away until their knees no longer touched, and it occurred to her that this awareness might not be one-sided. A pulse in her throat fluttered to life, and so did one low in her abdomen— a deep and insistent *throb-throb* that the rest of her body took up.

Dragging a breath into cramped lungs, she ordered herself to ignore it. They'd both made their positions clear. What was the point getting all hot and bothered when she couldn't do anything about it?

'Have I done anything wrong?' she asked, staring doggedly at the infuriatingly placid lake.

'Not wrong so much, as... It's just that a four-year-old doesn't fully understand yet the concept of keeping a secret.'

Blowing out a breath, she relaxed again.

'If Lili in her excitement should blurt out the secret to Marguerite, I would hate for you to be vexed with her.'

She reached out to touch his arm. 'Of course I won't be vexed.' She'd meant her touch to be a sign of reassurance. Instead, the power and heat of the man filtrated into her blood, making her want him with such an elemental fierceness she sucked in a breath. Snatching her hand back, she rubbed it against the linen of her trousers.

'Actually, Gabriel, I'm very much hoping she will let the cat out of the bag.'

That clenched hand on the table in front of him immediately loosened. He swung to her. 'You *want* Marguerite to find out?'

'Absolutely. She'd hate a surprise party, don't you think?'

'*Si.*'

'But a surprise party she knows about and can plan for...'

'You—'

He broke off, his face darkening, but she couldn't tell if it was in outrage or surprise.

'Think about it.' This time it was she who turned to him, though she was super careful not to bump him. 'This way Marguerite gets all the advantages of a surprise party, but with none of the drawbacks. Try your brownie.' It might help sweeten his mood.

With a disgruntled huff he bit into it, and as he slowly chewed, his eyelids lowered to half-mast with drowsy appreciation. Her breath caught. If she tasted him with the same lazy appreciation, would he—

Don't!

He sent her a sidelong glance from those grey eyes. 'You are a crafty harpy.'

'I'm not a *harpy*!' She feigned affront.

'A manoeuvrer then, a puller of strings.'

'But in a nice way.' She bit into her brownie, too, and groaned a little.

He gestured. 'Did you make these?'

She nodded. 'Nonna owned a restaurant and let me and my cousin Frankie help out in the school holidays. We loved it. Frankie adored being in the dining room with the customers—chatting and laughing and taking orders. But I loved to sneak into the kitchen and help out there.' It had been another haven.

He stared at her for a long moment. 'And Johanna? Did she love the restaurant, too?'

She loved that he asked, as if it'd be the most natural thing in the world that her sister would also be involved. 'Jo said nobody was tying her to a kitchen. She usually went away to camp during the school holidays—did far more exciting things like horse riding and kayaking.'

He laughed, and the sound of it made her feel happy and light, like she did when listening to her favourite pop music.

'Maria doesn't mind having you in her kitchen?'

'Not in the slightest. She understands that cooking can be a comfort. That it can help quieten the mind and soothe the soul.'

Intriguing lips pursed. She forced herself to look away.

'It has been a tempestuous time for you, yes? I had hoped the art would help, but—'

'Of course it's helped! Working here with you invigorates me. It fires me up—it's frustrating and satisfying in equal measure. But it's not *relaxing*. Do you find it relaxing?'

He opened his mouth, but closed it again with a frown. 'I find myself lost to it sometimes,' he finally said, 'and when I come back to myself, I am exhausted. But you are right. It is not relaxing. It is good that you have an outlet that is soothing and relaxing, too. Very good.'

'It's not the only one. Spending time with Lili is a delight.'

Something in his eyes lifted. 'Yes.'

'And with other members of the family, too.'

'With *the girls* as you call them?'

She nodded. 'And Marguerite.' Though she knew he wouldn't believe her. 'And I have hopes that the older members of the family will thaw as they get to know me better.'

He dragged a hand down his face, looking suddenly tired and grey. 'Have you approached Marguerite yet about setting up a foundation in Johanna's honour?'

Her chest clenched. 'I've mentioned it. She's thinking about it.' Forcing a smile, she lifted her chin. 'She'll come around, you'll see.' It would all work out.

'Audrey, you will be disappointed—'

'It's a risk I'm prepared to take.' She nodded at his abandoned brownie. 'Eat up. You call me a puller of strings, but you're wrong. I'm not pulling strings. I'm building bridges. I'm hoping that Marguerite knows by now that there's a surprise party in store for her—and that while I'm the brains behind it, the rest of the family is helping me in every way they can.'

'And what do you hope that will achieve?'

'Goodwill.'

'Audrey…'

She rushed on before he could pour cold water on her plans. 'And in the evenings that Marguerite and I spend together, I'm asking her advice about various family members.'

She watched him wrestle with his curiosity and saw the exact moment he surrendered to it, and it gave her a silly thrill of triumph. 'What kind of advice?'

'I asked her who I should set Livia up with. Do you know Livy hasn't dated since that awful sex scandal? No? Neither did Marguerite. I told her I thought it was dreadful what had happened, but that I didn't think it should put Livy off a relationship forever. Not all men are selfish jerks.'

'Did she suggest anyone?'

'Well, we discussed it long and hard because Livy needs someone kind-hearted and patient. We made a short list. I told her I'd get Tori and Ana's feedback, too, as they no doubt know these short-listed guys. I've told her I trust their judgement.'

His jaw dropped. 'You…'

'Bridge builder,' she provided for him. 'Also, Tori is thinking of starting up another business—she wants to help a community of women affected by domestic violence who've pooled their talents to make a range of funky T-shirts and earrings. Part of the proceeds go back into helping fund women's shelters. Tori's going to use her connections to create a more global platform for them.'

The pulse at the base of his throat throbbed. 'And Ana?'

She beamed at him. 'I'm glad you asked. Prior to her stint in rehab, she'd been working in her father's firm.'

He raked both hands back through his hair. 'You say *father's firm* like it's some kind of small holding. Audrey, it is one of the most prestigious real estate firms in all of Italy.'

'Whatever. The fact is she loved her job but her parents are so embarrassed at her downfall they'll barely speak to her, let alone give her old job back to her.'

'Yes, but—'

'She didn't steal from them, Gabriel. We all make mistakes. And we all deserve a second chance.'

'And this is the argument you presented to Marguerite?'

She bit into her brownie. 'I asked her advice for how we can best convince Ana's parents to give her her old job back.'

Autocratic lips twisted. 'I can already tell you how that went.'

'Go on, then.' She continued eating her brownie.

'If she didn't simply dismiss the idea and say it served Ana right.'

'Which she didn't.'

She licked her fingers clean of crumbs and Gabriel watched her as if mesmerised. Things inside her clenched up tight. He looked as if he'd like nothing more than to gobble her up. Shaking himself, he glared out at the water. Sagging, she seized her mug and buried her nose in it.

'Then she'd have said she would simply order Reggio and Claudia to give Adriana her job back.'

She nodded. That was exactly what Marguerite had said.

'What did you do?'

His voice was laden with doom and she couldn't help bristling a little. Why was he so sure she'd mess up and fall out of Marguerite's good graces?

'I didn't *do* anything. I simply laughed and told her I was starting to see why everyone was so terrified of her.'

His eyes widened and for a moment she could've sworn his lips twitched. 'What did she say?'

'She said that was *utter nonsense*. But I told her Nonna's motto had always been "You win more flies with honey than with vinegar."'

He choked on his coffee. 'You invoked your paternal grandmother?'

Admittedly, it had been a risk. But it had paid off. 'I suggested it might be better for domestic harmony—for Ana's relationship with her parents—if Marguerite made some throwaway comment about how well Ana seemed to be doing and suggested it might be time for her to get back to work, or something along those lines.'

'*Is* Adriana doing well?'

His face had closed up and it took a force of will not to seize what was left of her brownie and mash it against the front of his shirt. 'Of course she is! I don't lie, Gabriel. How many more times do we have to have this conversation?'

But the exhaustion that crossed his face tugged at her heart. Ana's drug addiction must remind him of Fina's. And anyone could see how badly Fina's death had marked him. How it still marked him.

'Sorry,' she murmured. 'I didn't mean to snap.'

'While I shouldn't have been so sceptical. I barely know Ana.'

She glared into her coffee. 'You hardly know any of them and yet you're happy to dismiss them wholesale as a bunch of hedonistic partygoers without a care for anyone but themselves and their own pleasure. Or in Marguerite's case that she'd sacrifice all for the family name. But you're wrong. The Funaros are like any other family—a complicated mix of good and bad. People aren't perfect, Gabriel, and it's unreasonable to expect them to not make mistakes.'

She wanted to add that what had happened to Fina wasn't anyone's fault—not his and not Marguerite's—but snapped her mouth shut. She'd already said more than she'd meant to.

'And this is what you are also trying to do between me and Marguerite—and the rest of the family—build a bridge?' Dark eyebrows rose over flinty eyes. 'You are trying to get me to see them in a different light.'

'I *would* like you to see them in a different light,' she admitted. 'A truer light.'

'Truer for whom?'

'I'm not being dishonest.' She crumpled her paper napkin. 'I'm not lying or making things up. Everything I tell you about Marguerite is the truth.'

'As *you* see it.'

'As I see it,' she agreed. 'In a way that isn't twisted by bitterness or hate.'

'If you should continue to attempt this thing, you will be making a mistake.'

He didn't speak with anger, but his quietness was ten times worse. She pressed fingers to her forehead. She would love for him and Marguerite to loosen their grip on the prejudices they held about each other.

'And then we will not be friends. I will not allow you to be my puppet master, Audrey.'

Her chin lifted. 'And are we friends?'

For the briefest of moments, stern lips relaxed into a smile. 'I am friendlier with you than I have ever before been with a Funaro.'

Not counting Fina, of course. Though that remained unspoken.

'I'm not manipulating anyone. I'm simply providing a vision of the truth that you are uncomfortable with, and I suspect Marguerite is, too, though she does a better job of hiding it. I believe you're a lot of things, Gabriel. I suspect you can be every bit as ruthless as Marguerite claims. But I also know you can be patient and kind. The one thing I didn't expect you to be was closed-minded.'

His jaw dropped.

'And from all you've lectured me on artistic practise, closed-mindedness is the death of art.'

If possible, his jaw dropped even farther.

She stood and planted her hands on her hips. 'Do you think I'm doing harm with this so-called string-pulling? Do you think I'm doing a bad thing? Do you think I am making a mess, making things worse?'

With a visible effort, he hauled his jaw into place. He neither glared nor yelled. Behind the grey of his eyes, she sensed his mind racing. Finally, he shook his head. 'You are trying to create harmony, and I think that in these instances—with *the girls*—you will succeed. You are looking after your friends. It is admirable. But I still think you are going to be disappointed.'

She sat again, tracked an eagle high above, circling on air currents. She kept her gaze trained on it. 'Why?'

'Because you are trying to create one big happy family here in Lake Como and that will never happen. You yearn so much for the love and security of family and are prepared to give your all for it, but you do not see how others can, and probably will, take advantage of that to promote their own agendas.'

She had to swallow. His perception—his recognition of her feelings about family—left her feeling raw and vulnerable. And yet, she wouldn't be as cynical as he was for all the world, even if the Funaros should end up breaking her heart.

'Or maybe they just need to experience someone loving them without an agenda, to understand what it's like to be loved unconditionally, to discover what it's worth. Maybe they need to be loved like that first, before they can see how they, too, can love like that.'

He swore under his breath. 'You need to develop some armour against the world, Audrey. You need—'

'I don't see your armour bringing you any joy, Gabriel, so excuse me if I don't jump on board your armour train. You are dismissing vulnerability as something to be afraid of. You don't understand what a gift it can be. Armour?' She snorted. 'Armour simply weighs one down.'

Gabriel watched Audrey return to the studio with her plate and mug, her shoulders back and her head held high, and an icy fist reached inside his chest and squeezed.

She had such faith in people. What would happen when this family took all she had to give then stomped all over her? Who and what would she turn to for solace when they refused to live up to her expectations and behaved their worst—when she felt discarded and unloved and betrayed?

She enjoyed the finest French champagne now, but would she start chugging back bottles of the stuff to take the edge off the pain? Would she lose herself to a string of love affairs and one-night stands in an effort to find a physical release from her sadness and sense of failure? Would she turn to drugs…?

Breathing hard, he ran a hand over his face. He and Lili would be there for her, and so would her art, but would it be enough? What else could he give her that would provide some comfort if this came tumbling down around her ears?

If? Don't you mean when?

Tapping fingers against the table, he realized that if things truly did go badly, he wasn't sure she'd know how to get away from the villa. Marguerite could stymie a cab driver, refuse them entrance. His lips pressed into a tight line. That at least was something he could help with.

Seizing his mug and plate, he, too, returned to the studio. 'Audrey, do you know how to drive?'

She glanced around from *Ties That Bind*. He thought she'd finished it.

'I have an Australian driver's licence, but I've not driven in Italy yet.' She shuddered. 'You guys drive on the wrong side of the road.'

He ignored the shudder. 'Would you like to learn to drive here?'

She turned around fully. 'Are you offering to teach me?'

'*Si.*'

'Why?'

'I think it is wise for every person to have as much independence as possible.' He would do for her what he'd never thought to do for Fina.

'You think there might be a situation in the future where I'll need to make a quick getaway?'

Her lips twitched as if she found him amusing. He didn't care. She could be amused all she liked as long as she was also prepared. 'It is better to be safe than sorry.'

She stared at him for several long moments, but

to his relief, finally nodded. 'I'd very much like to practise my driving with someone capable. As you say, you never know when such a skill might come in handy. Thank you for the offer.'

Excellent. He gestured at *Ties That Bind*. 'I thought you had finished.'

'I did, too, but something in me refused to rest. And it just occurred to me that one can lift off my frame and the figure beneath is suddenly freed, but…that's not the truth of the piece. It's not the way things work in the real world. So now I want to send threads from here to here—' she pointed '—and here to here. So that it is all fully integrated. I know it will make the piece harder to transport. That two pieces now become one, but…' She shrugged.

He stared at the piece, and as always, things inside him clenched.

'Are you sure the figure there trapped behind that beautiful web is not you?' He wasn't sure he could stand it if that was how she felt.

'I don't feel trapped, Gabriel.'

He tried to feel relief, but it wouldn't come. 'Who *is* the figure, then?'

She frowned. 'Why does it have to be anyone?'

Because every instinct he had told him she'd created that piece with someone particular in mind. Johanna? Marguerite?

Before he could ask, her frown deepened. 'Who was the figure in *Maybe*? Who was your muse for that piece?'

'Fina.'

She flinched and it had him refocusing fully on her rather than her artwork. She stared at him with wide eyes, the colour draining from her face. How was it possible for her to grieve so hard for the dead sister she'd never known? Exhaustion swamped him and he dropped into the nearest chair. 'It was when I didn't know if she was going to overcome her addiction or give in to it completely.'

It had been during her second stint in rehab. He'd had such high hopes. They hadn't been realised, and even now the acrid taste of disappointment burned his throat.

Audrey gave a low laugh, but it held no humour. His every sense was on high alert.

'*That's* what me sitting for you has been about?'

Her mouth twisted in self-derision, as if she'd been a fool. He found himself on his feet. 'What do you mean?'

She paced the long length of the bench running the width of the room. 'You haven't wanted me to sit for you because of who I am, because there's something about *me* that speaks to you.' She thumped a hand to her chest.

What the hell...?

She swung around, eyes flashing. 'I've just been a substitute for your real muse—*Fina!*'

She had this wrong. *So* wrong.

'I thought your creative block was because you'd been trapped in your grief for so long that you'd forgotten how to have fun and enjoy yourself. I thought I'd somehow helped to pull you out of that funk—that in agreeing to be your student, I'd given you a different focus.' She flung an arm in the air. 'I thought having a female role model for Lili—a woman who would love her—had helped quieten some of your fears. I thought those things combined—'

She broke off, breathing hard. 'God, I must have an ego the size—' she gestured out the window '—of a lake!'

The magnitude of her misapprehension left him speechless. He tried to make his brain work; tried to formulate words to tell her how mistaken she was.

'Instead, all of this time I've been a substitute, a very sad second best, but a chance nonetheless for you to relive your glory days with Fina.'

The expression in her eyes pierced him to the very core.

'No wonder you didn't want to be friends. Were so intent on keeping me at a distance. You didn't want to bring the temporary fantasy that Fina still lived crashing down.'

'You are so wrong!'

The shouted words reverberated around the studio, reaching into the farthest, darkest corners.

'Incredibly, stupendously and momentously *wrong*!' he roared.

Her head rocked back.

He stabbed a finger at her. 'I hadn't been married to Fina a full year before I realised what a mistake our marriage was.'

The shock in her eyes was far more welcome than the previous self-loathing.

'I wanted a divorce.'

Her hand flew to her mouth.

'But then Fina became pregnant and…' He raised his arms, let them drop back to his sides. 'I hoped things would change. We had made vows. It is wrong to give up on a marriage without a fight. I wanted to be there for Fina and I wanted to be there for our child.'

Neither of them said anything for several long moments.

'My relationship with Fina was not the great romance you seem to think it.'

She took several steps towards him. 'You must've loved her once.'

'She didn't marry me because she loved me. She married me as an act of rebellion…because she knew Marguerite would not approve.'

She moved another step closer. 'But *you* must've loved *her*.'

'I must've done,' he agreed. 'But I cannot remember feeling that way now. All I remember is her destructiveness and her selfishness, and how I wished to break free of her. You are wrong, Audrey. I am not mired in grief.' He was mired in guilt. He did what he could to get his raging emotions back under control. 'However, Lili has lost her mother, and that is a great tragedy.'

'I'm sorry,' she offered quietly.

He moved across until they stood toe to toe. 'You have not been a sad substitute. You do not, thankfully, remind me of Fina in any fashion. You are ten times the woman she was.'

Her lips parted and she blinked.

He leaned down until they were eye to eye, the cleanness of her scent welling up all around him. 'I keep my distance because I am the one who demanded there be no romantic entanglement between us. And yet, when you are near, all I can think about is kissing you.'

Her throat bobbed and her gaze lowered to his lips, clove-coloured eyes darkening to walnut. 'So…' That gaze returned to his and she swallowed again. 'I haven't imagined that?'

His hands clenched to fists to stop from reaching for her. 'You haven't imagined it.' He would not undermine her confidence or sense of self the way Fina had his, no matter what the admission might cost him.

'And you know I feel the same way. That sometimes I look at you and—'

'Yes!' He cut her off before her words could inflame him further.

'So…it's safer to keep our distance.'

He tried to push another yes from his throat, but it wouldn't come.

She moistened her lips. 'What would happen if we broke those rules?' She said the words as if to herself. 'Would the sky fall in?' The pulse in her throat fluttered. It took all his strength not to lower his head and touch his lips to the spot. 'Should we amend the rules?'

This was madness, but as he stared at the line of her throat, took in the oversized man's button-down shirt she wore when she worked, the vee of the neckline hinting at shadowed cleavage, hunger roared through him. 'Amend the rules how?' The words rasped out of him.

'I still don't want a boyfriend. But I've never wanted a man the way I want you. What I feel for you is…*greedy*. I've been careful my whole life not to be greedy, but I see you and I want…'

She reached out and placed her hand on his chest. The warmth of her hand penetrated the thin cotton of his T-shirt and he sucked in a breath. 'And you want what?' he demanded.

She met his gaze and her eyes widened—at whatever she saw in his face or her own audacity, he had no idea.

'I want to claw off your clothes and feast on you, and have you feast on me. I want to be greedy.'

She spoke clearly, as if she wanted her every word to hit him with the force of a mini tornado. He couldn't move. If he did, he'd kiss her, and there'd be no going back.

'Can I kiss you, Gabriel?'

His body shook from the force of holding back. 'If we kiss, Audrey, we will not stop.' He reached out and pulled the clip from her hair. Her hair fell past her shoulders and he wrapped his hand around it, pulled her head back until her throat was exposed to him. He pressed a kiss there, grazed the sensitive skin with his teeth and she whimpered. The sound arrowed to his groin.

'Release my hair, Gabriel.'

He didn't want to, but he did as she asked. Rather than move away, though, she hooked a hand behind his head and drew his face down to hers, her eyes glittering and her breath shallow. 'We keep it here, at the studio. We don't take it back to the villa or anywhere else. Agreed?'

His heart beat so hard he thought she must hear it. 'Agreed.'

Bunching her fingers in his shirt, she dragged it over his head and then simply stared at him. 'Can I change my mind? Can I ask you to sit for me naked?'

'You can have me however you want.'

And then they were tearing at each other's clothes. It was raw and physical and primal. He wanted to slow it down, but she wouldn't let him. She seemed to know exactly how to touch him to inflame him and make him forget himself.

'Now,' she demanded, sobbing when he touched her in that most intimate of places. She was soft and wet and ready. Wrapping a hand around him, she squeezed gently and he bucked into her hand. 'Now, Gabriel, now!' she demanded. 'I want you inside me *now*.'

He went to sweep the bench clear, but it would mean disturbing her current embroidery.

He swung away to the other bench. 'We'll hurt your work,' she groaned.

Stumbling together, they hit the back wall. He took the force before swinging them around and lifting her up, her back braced against the wall as he fumbled with a condom from his wallet on the bench. Her legs wrapped around his waist and he lowered her down. They both shook as she closed around him.

They stilled, staring at each other. It felt as if not just time but the world itself stopped, and then they were moving with a greedy fervour that shook him to his core. They moved with a mutual rhythm, not once breaking stride, not once falling out of step.

Her breaths, her moans and whimpers filled his ears. Her cries as her muscles tightened and she broke around him. His name on her lips.

From somewhere far off a guttural cry sounded—him?—and then he was sucked into a swirling vortex of pleasure that shook every atom of his body with its force—breaking and then rearranging it in a different pattern.

And leaving him feeling like a new man.

CHAPTER ELEVEN

As GABRIEL LOWERED her feet to the floor, Audrey wondered if her legs would hold her upright. *Good legs.* She praised them when they did. *Very good legs.*

Not that he let her go. They were both breathing hard. She had one arm flung around his neck; the other drifted down to rest against his ample chest. He'd wrapped one strong arm around her waist and his forehead rested beside her on the wall.

Closing her eyes, she did what she could to catch her breath. That had been…*intense*.

Eventually, Gabriel roused himself and swore softly. 'Did I hurt you?'

Her eyes flew open and she reached up to touch his face. 'You took me to heaven.'

Grey eyes met hers. He traced a finger down her cheek. 'I lost all control. You probably have bruises on your back.'

'And you probably have scratch marks on yours.' She bit her lip. 'I might've even drawn blood.'

He smiled. And it was sweet and warm and every good thing. Things inside her melted and begged and did all manner of things she couldn't begin to decipher when her mind was still so full of him, and while he remained so close.

She needed him to stay close. She didn't want him moving just yet.

'I loved your enthusiasm,' he murmured, pushing her hair from her face. 'I loved how much you wanted me.' His gaze darkened. 'You made me feel alive again.'

He'd made her feel like a wild woman. 'I didn't know it could be that good,' she whispered.

His gaze roved her face and he nodded as if in approval. 'I have dreamed of seeing you mussed like this, and it is every bit as beguiling as I knew it would be. You are an extraordinary woman, Audrey.'

She melted some more, cupped his face and kissed him. A warm kiss that he returned with the same goodwill that threaded through her.

'I meant to savour you, though.'

She bit her lip and drew back a fraction, curiosity rippling through her. What did he mean by that?

'I meant to take it slow, meant to explore every inch of your body, learning what gave you pleasure, taking my time until you were begging for release.'

Warmth flushed through her cheeks. And other places. 'What? *Now, Gabriel, now. Please!* wasn't enough begging for you?'

His chuckle warmed her all the way through. 'Next time,' he promised. 'I am afraid I will not want to do any work if we are keeping this thing here and only here.'

'It has to stay here.' They both knew it.

It had to stay here, because if they took this thing into the real world, she was afraid she'd fall in love with him. As long as they kept it within these four walls it would continue to feel like nothing more than an escapist dream, a flight of fancy—something not quite real.

Gabriel didn't want her falling in love with him. Marguerite didn't want her falling in love with him, either. An icy drip slid down her spine, and she wasn't masochistic enough to set herself up for that kind of heartache.

Gabriel would never fall in love with her. She was a Funaro, and that was something he'd never be able to overlook. He might make her body sing, but she'd be a fool to expect more. If he thought her feelings were getting involved, he'd walk away without a backwards glance—perhaps tossing her one of those blisteringly sardonic smiles over his shoulder first.

She shivered, and he rubbed his hands up and down her arms. 'Are you cold?'

Pulling in a breath, she smiled. 'No, I'm fine.'

Nobody would fall in love with anybody. They'd keep things light, they'd keep them fun...and they'd keep them separate. They'd enjoy each other, be kind to each other and remain friends when this eventually ended. Because regardless of anything else, she did feel that finally they were friends.

Over the next week Gabriel introduced Audrey to a brand-new world of sensuality. He showed her exactly what he intended when he'd said he'd meant to savour her. He made her beg as he promised he would. He made her soar. He made her feel replete. He made her feel *complete*.

In turn, she savoured him with the same slow relish; learned all she could about his body and what gave him pleasure. It made her want to pinch herself to know she had the power to affect him so greatly. To see that masculine body trembling at her touch. She made him beg, too; made him lose control...made him soar.

'How long before it burns itself out?' she asked after a particularly earth-shattering session of lovemaking. Her hand trailed a path across his naked chest as they lay on the bed in the mezzanine level he'd revealed to her the afternoon of the first day they'd become lovers. The view outside that enormous wall of glass was as spectacular as ever, but it was the man who captured her attention and held it.

'I do not know.' His fingers traced delicate patterns across her back. She wondered if she could capture those patterns and this feeling in an embroidery. 'You wish to be tired of me already?'

'Absolutely not!' But in a far-off corner of her mind, she hoped the need and intensity would soon lessen. At the villa they tried to avoid each other. Oh, she spent time with Lili, but he no longer accompanied her. They might have rules about where and when and how they could indulge their explosive chemistry, but their bodies had minds of their own.

And refused to be ruled.

The driving lessons he insisted on giving her were a special form of torture. But neither of them broke the promise they'd made. Even though she could see in the set of his jaw, the pulse in his throat and the fire in his eyes that he wanted her every bit as much as she wanted him.

'We are friends now, Gabriel, yes?'

He lifted up on one elbow, a frown in his eyes. 'Of course. I like you. I care about you.' He blinked as if the admission surprised him. 'Do you doubt it?'

She shook her head. 'I feel it in here.' She touched her chest. A hungry light came into his eyes as he glanced at her chest, making her swallow. 'I just wanted to make sure you felt it, too. Gabriel…' She hesitated. 'You know I've no desire to hurt or vex you?'

His frown deepened. 'I trust you, if that is what you ask. Why?'

'Because I want you to tell me more about Fina. What happened? How did she die?'

He sat up, a mix of emotions racing across his face as he settled back against the headboard.

She sat up, too, but rather than rest beside him, she curled against his chest, her head nestled beneath his chin, and she let out a sigh of relief when, after a moment's hesitation, his arm went around her.

'I know this sounds silly. I mean, I didn't even know I had a sister until a few weeks ago. But now that I do—not having had a chance to meet her, know her, makes me feel as if a part of me is missing.'

'Audrey.' Her name was nothing more than a murmured sigh, and when she glanced up, the tired expression in his face pricked her heart. 'Do you have this image in your mind of a lovely, warm woman with whom you could've been best friends?'

She let out a breath. 'Not anymore.'

'The things I tell you won't make you like her very much.'

'And yet they'll be the truth. And that's what I want—the truth.'

She watched him war with himself. She settled back against his chest. 'Please?' she whispered.

'Where to even start,' he murmured.

'At the beginning.' She kept her voice soft, though she wasn't sure why. 'How did you meet?'

'We were both living in Rome at the time. We met at one of my exhibitions. When I saw her—it was as if someone had punched the breath from my body. I had never met anyone more vibrant. She was very beautiful, very charismatic...and so confident.'

'She bowled you over.'

'Completely. Ours was a whirlwind romance. We were married within six months of meeting. I have never been a rash man, and yet I rushed into that marriage without thinking twice. I didn't notice—or didn't want to notice—that she was also headstrong and reckless. I thought they were simply factors of being a Funaro and that once she married, she would settle down.'

'That's not what happened?'

She glanced up to see him shake his head. 'At first, I was happy to attend the parties and society functions that she so loved, but the novelty eventually wore off. I had commissions to fill and wanted to get back to work. She kept promising we'd move to Milan, near to her family, and start living a quieter life. But that day never seemed to come. That's when I realised we barely knew one another.'

'What did you do?'

'I hired studio space in Rome so I could at least work, and then set out to woo my wife—to make her truly fall in love with me. I didn't care where we lived, but I wanted to spend time with her. And I wanted her to spend time with me.'

'That didn't turn out the way you wanted?'

Doh! Clearly, it hadn't.

He gave a mirthless laugh. 'Oh, she was more than happy to have me in her bed, but it didn't stop her partying. It didn't stop the excessive drinking or the recreational drugs.'

She winced.

'And then she became pregnant. I hoped rather than believed things would change. I seized on the opportunity to settle us into a different routine— away from the drinking and drugs. We bought a villa on the outskirts of Milan, which she spent a fortune redecorating and furnishing.'

'And were you happy?' She wanted them to have had at least a taste of happiness before it all went so terribly wrong.

He was silent for several long minutes. 'We'd moved to Milan to be closer to her family. It was where she'd grown up. I foolishly thought she would appreciate having them near, to have their support during her pregnancy, but she missed her social life in Rome. She started throwing lavish parties, which I attended to make sure she didn't drink or take drugs while pregnant. Funnily enough, she didn't seem to mind that, and the parties kept her entertained for a while. But then she became...'

'What?'

'Resentful of the changes in her body.'

She couldn't hide her dismay.

One powerful shoulder lifted. 'I did what I could to reassure her...'

The set of his jaw and the expression in his eyes told her how that had played out.

'She went into self-imposed seclusion until Lili was born. Shut herself away, refused to see anyone, including Marguerite. She'd barely talk to me—blaming me for the state she found herself in. I hired a team of doctors and nurses and they did everything they could.'

Fina had taken no joy in her pregnancy? Audrey sagged against him. It should've been one of the most joyful and exciting times of her life.

'I had heard of postpartum depression, of course. What I hadn't known is that seven percent of pregnant women also suffer from depression.'

'And Fina was one of them.'

He shrugged. 'Or maybe she was simply a selfish brat who hated anyone or anything curtailing her freedom.'

Whoa!

'Why do you say that?' she asked carefully.

'Because as soon as Lili was born, and she'd lost the pregnancy weight, she immediately started partying again. She had absolutely no interest in the baby, and when I confronted her about it, she told me that in birthing a new Funaro heiress, she'd performed her duty. And that if I didn't want the bother of a child then to hire a nanny.'

Her hand flew to her mouth.

'That was the moment I realised what a spoiled young woman Fina was. It was the moment I realised that she cared nothing for either Lili or me.'

She wrapped an arm around his waist, hugged him tight. 'I'm sorry, Gabriel.'

'She moved back to Rome, started drinking again, taking drugs…and lovers. While I started getting legal advice about a divorce and getting custody of Lili. I wanted nothing more to do with Fina. I hated her for disregarding Lili like she had, for dismissing her as if she was worth nothing. Marguerite, of course, caught wind of what I was planning and we had an awful row. She blamed me for Fina's fecklessness and I blamed her.'

Audrey winced.

'But she convinced me to come to Rome with her to confront Fina together. And then there was another row. That was when I discovered Fina had married me to spite Marguerite. I hadn't known until then that Marguerite had been against the match. I left without a backwards glance. Headed back to the lawyers in Milan. But before I could start divorce proceedings, Fina died. She'd been partying on a yacht off the coast of Portofino, had taken a cocktail of party drugs and slipped overboard. A couple of people saw her fall and raised the alarm, but they were terribly inebriated and by the time Fina was found, it was too late. She'd drowned.'

Audrey closed her eyes. Just as Gabriel had said, Fina had self-destructed.

He'd fallen headlong in love with Fina and he'd never be that unguarded again…that *wholehearted* in his emotions. The thought had her aching for him, even as a chill crept over her.

Would there be a price to pay for these stolen moments?

Don't be foolish.

This thing they shared wasn't love. It was… pleasure, respite, fun.

Actually, it felt a lot like family—the sense of belonging, the no need to be on one's guard, to be with someone with honesty and trust. It was what she'd had with Jo, Nonna, Aunt Deidre and Frankie. When this thing between them had run its course, she and Gabriel would still have that.

'The coroner said there were so many drugs in

her system that she'd probably lost consciousness before she hit the water.'

And just like that, a young woman had lost her life. She shivered.

'I'm sorry, Audrey.' He rubbed her arm as if to warm her. 'It's a far from edifying story.'

'But I wanted to know. And I'm glad to know. Thank you for telling me.' She rubbed her cheek against his chest, welcoming his warmth. 'I don't think Fina and I would've become friends.'

'No.'

'I think she must've been a terribly unhappy person to act the way she did.'

'I agree.'

'But her unhappiness stemmed from a time before she met you.' She struggled into a sitting position. 'You do know that, don't you?'

He nodded.

Subsiding back against the headboard, they both stared out at the view, but things inside her continued to throb. 'Gabriel, all of that is in the past now. It happened two years ago, but as you just said, you and Fina were over long before then. Why haven't you met someone else? You're young and virile.'

And so alone.

She hated the thought of him with someone else. But she hated the thought of him being alone more.

'You listen to my ugly story and you don't judge any of us, but perhaps you should. None of us are nice people.'

'That's not true!' He'd been kind to her—gruff at times, stern, even unfriendly, but still kind. He was a generous lover. And he adored his daughter. He was a good man.

'If I had tried harder, if I might've seen beneath Fina's recklessness to the unhappy young woman she really was, I could've helped her. Instead, I let pride and hurt feelings override what I knew in my gut—that if she continued on her path, she would die an early death.'

Even though he spoke the truth, his words cut him like knives. Shoving the sheet back, he pulled on a pair of shorts and strode to the railing, not really seeing the view spread in front of him.

'It was your mother, Danae, who got her onto drugs. Did you know that? She abandoned Fina when she was two years old and didn't return until Fina was sixteen.'

'I thought Danae returned to her family here after she left Australia.'

Danae, another troubled Funaro heiress, had taken recklessness to new heights. He turned to meet Audrey's gaze. She reclined against the headboard, those walnut eyes watching him, and his body tightened and hardened at the sight. 'According to the rest of the family, she would never say where she'd been or what she'd been up to. She was missing for thirteen years, and when she came home she refused to act the mother to sixteen-year-old Fina, taking instead the role of the rebellious older sister.'

She leaned towards him. 'But to introduce your own daughter to drugs? What kind of person does that?'

'She left less than a year after she'd returned. I can see now how much that marked Fina.'

'To have your mother come back into your life simply to leave again. Poor Fina. She must've felt doubly abandoned. As if she were somehow not enough.'

It took all his strength not to flinch at her words. She hadn't uttered them as an accusation, but it was what he deserved—to be held accountable.

'I never met Danae. I found out only after Fina died what had happened to her.'

'What did happen to her?'

He didn't want to answer, but if anyone deserved the truth, it was Audrey. 'She took some mind-altering drug while she was away travelling…it addled her brain.'

'She died of a drug overdose?'

He rubbed a hand over his face. 'She's not dead, Audrey. But her mind is lost. She's in a private clinic north of here on the Swiss border.'

She shot out of bed to stand in front of him. '*Not* dead?'

He forced himself to look at her. 'It's the Funaro family's greatest secret, and most of them don't know it.'

'But Marguerite told me she was dead.'

'She might as well be. Her body lives on, but… If you were to visit her, she'd not know you.'

'I don't want to visit her.' She dropped to the bed as if her legs would no longer hold her up. 'Did Fina know the truth?'

'No.'

She buried her face in her hands. Long moments passed, but she eventually pulled them away, her eyes murky with sorrow. 'And as a result, Marguerite bears the same burden of guilt that you do.'

He stabbed a finger at her. 'Fina should've been told the truth!'

'Because maybe then she'd have avoided taking drugs to ensure the same thing didn't happen to her?'

Yes! 'I should've known the truth!' If he'd known the truth, maybe he'd—

What? mocked an ugly voice. *Tried harder?*

He hadn't been able to get away from Fina fast enough. *That* was the truth. He hadn't *wanted* to try harder.

Wheeling around, he gripped the railing with all his strength. Feeling the weight of his own culpability. 'It is true that I blame Marguerite. But I married Fina. I was supposed to look after her. I failed her, and because of that Lili no longer has a mother and—'

'Stop it.' Warm arms slid around his waist. 'You aren't to blame for the choices Fina made. Neither is Marguerite. And if we want to be brutally honest, neither is Danae.'

Outrage made him turn, but one look at her face and he didn't have the heart to break away.

'Fina was an adult, Gabriel. A grown woman in charge of her own destiny. She had other options available to her to deal with her problems. She didn't have to turn to drugs. She made bad choices.' Her grip tightened, urging him to meet her gaze. 'Did you suggest counselling? Drug rehabilitation?'

'Of course I did. I—'

'You couldn't drag her there against her will, though. She needed to make that decision of her own free will. You couldn't impose it on her—no matter how much you wanted to save her.'

He hated her words at the same time as he hungered to believe them.

She cupped his face in both her hands, her eyes swimming with unshed tears. 'If Fina's daughter couldn't save her, Gabriel, you and Marguerite didn't stand a chance. And all of this guilt and regret, it's eating you alive. You need to let it go.'

She stood there offering him a vision of a future he didn't dare believe in. Reaching up on tiptoe, she kissed him, and he kissed her back with a need he could barely temper, wanting to lose himself in her warmth and softness and belief. She opened up to him without reservation and he took everything she gave, searching for peace and release... and absolution.

* * *

'Tomorrow is Thursday.' Thursday was one of the days Audrey didn't work at the studio.

She glanced around from pulling on the cotton sundress over her head, and Gabriel wanted to pull it back over her head, drag her back to bed and make love with her all over again. But the afternoon shadows were starting to lengthen and he would need to take her back to the villa soon.

'We've barely worked these last two weeks.'

They'd both tried to settle to their respective works in progress, and Audrey had even started a new piece, but their hunger for each other had yet to subside, and their concentration for anything work related never lasted long. 'If you wanted to come here with me tomorrow…' he offered now.

Her eyes danced. 'But would we work?'

Righting her dress, she surveyed him reclining on the bed completely naked and swallowed. A smile built inside him. He revelled in the way just the sight of him could undo her. He stretched and sent her a lazy grin.

Her breath hitched and she gave a shaky laugh. 'You stop that right now, Gabriel Matteo Dimarco!'

He loved it that she called him by his full name when she was trying to be stern with him.

'Up!' She made shooing gestures with her hands before throwing his jeans at him. 'Get dressed.'

'Why the hurry?'

'It's Wednesday night.'

Some of the brightness bled from the day. Wednesday night was the one night of the week Marguerite demanded Lili spend at the villa rather than in the cottage with him. Though if Lili was otherwise occupied...

'Would you like to come to the cottage tonight?'

She froze.

'I could cook for you.' He would like to do that. 'And—'

'I can't.'

Her voice sounded strangled and he frowned, but then she smiled and he thought he must've imagined it. But something chafed at him; something he couldn't explain. After rolling out of bed, he dragged on his jeans.

'It's date night with Lili and Marguerite.'

Standing on opposite sides of the bed, they made it, smoothing out the creases and fluffing up the pillows and the duvet until it looked smooth and fresh, as if they'd never been there. He immediately wanted to mess it up again. Mess her up and convince her to change her plans for him tonight.

Audrey stared at him across the divide of the bed. 'We agreed to keep things here, at the studio.'

'Would it matter if we stole a few extra moments elsewhere?'

'Yes.'

'Why?'

She hesitated.

'Audrey?'

'I don't want Marguerite knowing about us.'

Ice crept across his scalp. He recalled that fight between Fina and Marguerite.

I loved how much it irked you when I married a lowbred, impoverished artist. The expression on your face when you discovered I was pregnant by him. It was worth the price I had to pay.'

His nostrils flared. His hands clenched. 'I'm fine to sleep with just as long as nobody knows. Is that it? I lack the polish the Funaros are renowned for and you don't want to be sullied by association. You'd—'

'If that's what you think, then you don't know me at all!'

Her eyes flashed, and shame, hot and hard, hit him in the gut. Audrey wasn't Fina.

'We agreed to keep this thing between us here where it's contained and…not real. Once we take it into the everyday world, it becomes *real*. And if it becomes real it'll lead to complications.' She strode around the bed to poke him in the chest with a hard finger. 'Do you want complications, Gabriel? Because I was under the impression you didn't.'

He didn't want complications. He'd do anything to avoid those. Reaching out, he cupped her face, lowered his brow to hers. 'I am sorry. I know you are not like that. It was an appalling thing to say. Please forgive me.'

She gave a funny little hiccup. 'Why did you say it, then?'

'Frustration.' He couldn't seem to get enough of her. 'Jealousy that you're spending tonight with someone else rather than with me in my bed.' He released her with a frown. 'What happens on Wednesday nights anyway?' The words growled out of him but he couldn't help it. 'It seems as if it's some top-secret thing. It makes me suspicious. Whenever I ask Lili she says it's a girls' night.'

'Because that's what it is—a girls' night.'

Was Audrey in on this, too? Were she and Marguerite in cahoots…?

To what? He was being paranoid.

He frowned again. He had every right to be paranoid where Marguerite was concerned. She—

'If we're really friends, Gabriel, then you shouldn't mind spending time with me outside of the bedroom.'

Her words had him stiffening. 'Of course I enjoy spending time with you doing other things!' He looked forward to their driving expeditions, even though his body hungered for her the entire time. He enjoyed the conversations they had after their lovemaking, or over coffee during their breaks. He enjoyed working side by side with her. 'I value you for more than just the sex, Audrey.

You must not doubt that.' He wanted her to understand that she was valuable to him on many levels.

She stuck out her hip. 'Then join us for our
girls' night tonight. But if you agree, you have to
understand that for the evening, you are an honorary girl. And you are not allowed to criticise proceedings or to have an opinion on what happens.'

His eyes narrowed, his suspicion radar pinging
madly. 'How is it possible to not have an opinion?'

She pursed her lips. 'Okay, that's true. Then you
need to agree to keep your opinions to yourself.'

Could he do that? If he didn't, it would earn
her a big black mark in Marguerite's books. He
might not like Marguerite, but he knew what family meant to Audrey and he wouldn't do anything
to damage that.

He gave one hard nod. 'You have a deal.' He
would take this chance to enter the inner sanc-
tum and judge for himself if Marguerite was lead-
ing his daughter astray, putting pressure on her
to conform to a certain image and behaviour,
and grooming her for a life of a socialite when he
wanted so much more for her.

As directed, Gabriel turned up at the villa at 6 p.m.
on the dot. Audrey met him with a smile and led
him upstairs and down several corridors he'd never
ventured along before. Opening a door, she led him
into...

A media room.

He couldn't have said why, but it was the last thing he'd expected. An enormous TV took up most of one wall, and four sets of three-seater sofas rested in front of it—the second row slightly raised like in a theatre. Each seat had cupholders, a table in the arm that pulled out, and each seat reclined.

'Here's our mystery guest,' Audrey announced.

Marguerite glanced up, partially hidden by a drinks cabinet, and rolled her eyes, but remained mercifully silent. Lili bounced up and down. 'Papa! You're a girl tonight.'

'I am,' he agreed gravely.

'I get to decide where everyone sits—that's my job—because I'm Princess Lili.'

His lips twitched. 'And where would Princess Lili like me to sit?'

She cocked her head to one side. 'Tonight I'm sitting here.' She pointed to the middle seat of one of the front sofas. 'Princess Nonna is sitting here.' She pointed to the seat on the right of hers and Marguerite immediately took it. 'Princess Audrey's seat is here.' Audrey sat in the seat Lili pointed to on her other side. 'And Princess Papa,' she giggled. 'You get a whole sofa to yourself.' She pointed to the sofa directly behind her. He immediately moved to it because the others had taken their seats so quickly and he didn't want to get the etiquette wrong and spoil Lili's fun.

A knock sounded on the door. Lili knelt on her seat to face him. 'That'll be the pizza.'

Pizza? Marguerite was eating pizza?

'It's Audrey's job to order the pizza and Nonna's job to serve the drinks.'

Had he entered an alternate universe? He watched Audrey race to the door to take the pizza boxes from one of the maids and realised she wore her oldest jeans.

In front of Marguerite!

Marguerite moved to the drinks cabinet again. And he realised she wore a... Good God, the woman was wearing a tracksuit. While Lili was in her pyjamas.

'What would Princess Lili and Princess Audrey like to drink?' Marguerite enquired in her beautifully modulated voice. He felt as if he'd stepped into an alternate reality.

'Lemonade, please,' Audrey said.

'Orange juice, please,' Lili said.

'Princess Papa...' He could've sworn Marguerite uttered that with relish. 'What would you like to drink? We have sodas as well as orange, apple or pineapple juice.'

He'd kill for a beer, but that clearly wasn't on offer. 'A cola please... Princess Marguerite,' he couldn't help adding, and could've sworn the older woman's lips twitched.

Audrey handed around paper napkins and plates

loaded with pizza. 'Tonight I chose a vegetarian pizza and a pepperoni pizza.'

'Lovely.' Marguerite passed around the drinks in cups with straws in them. Had he ever seen her drink out of anything but crystal or fine bone china?

With a wink in his direction, Audrey settled into her seat. 'What movie are we watching tonight, Princess Lili?'

'Ready?' Lili lifted the remote and pressed Play.

'Ooh, *Ever After.*' Marguerite rubbed her hands together as the opening credits rolled.

'I love this movie.' Audrey grinned at Lili. 'I love me a feisty Cinderella.'

'Me, too.' Lili nodded twice, even though he doubted she knew what the word meant. 'Can I be Feisty Princess Lili next week?'

'I think we should all be Feisty Princesses next Wednesday night,' Marguerite said.

Audrey nodded. 'Yes, let's.'

He watched in amazement as the three women— *princesses*—ate pizza, drank their juices and watched a fairy-tale movie with pure and easy enjoyment. Watched as Lili curled up first against her grandmother, and then eventually fell asleep in Audrey's lap.

He felt like Alice when she tumbled down the rabbit hole.

CHAPTER TWELVE

'I THINK THIS is where I say I told you so,' Audrey said as she passed a plate of thinly sliced ham to her grandmother the next morning at breakfast.

'I take it you're referring to our special guest last night?' Marguerite took a slice of wafer-thin ham and set it neatly on her plate.

That was one of the things she most loved about her grandmother—she didn't feign ignorance; wasn't the slightest bit coy. 'It wasn't dreadful or awkward or any of the things you were concerned about, was it?' She hadn't misread her grandmother's serenity of the night before, had she? Marguerite had still enjoyed their girls' night.

'You were right, Audrey, and I'm glad of it. Gabriel wasn't all bristling resentment as I expected.' She cut a small portion of ham and chewed it thoughtfully. 'He's a good father. It's something I never doubted. I'm glad he can put aside his own feelings to present a good face for Lili's benefit. It will be much easier for her, if her father and I can appear friendly when we're around each other.'

'It'd be best for Lili if the two of you actually stopped being so stubborn and got to know each other properly. I'm convinced that if you did, you'd become the best of friends.'

'My dear Audrey, it's best not to wish for the moon.' Marguerite eyed her from the head of the table. 'You aren't getting too attached to Gabriel, are you?'

Something weird and hot squirmed through her, but she ignored it. 'He's become a friend—a good friend. I appreciate all he's done for me. I appreciate the fact he's promoted my relationship with Lili. And—' She broke off with a frown.

'And?' Marguerite raised an eyebrow.

She blew out a breath. 'Well, he's blisteringly honest at times, which can be confronting.'

Marguerite set her cutlery down. 'Has he hurt you?'

She sent her grandmother a swift smile. 'He hurt my feelings *dreadfully* when he called a particular piece I was working on *derivative*. I had to take a little walk along the waterfront to calm down.'

Marguerite's lips twitched.

'To make matters worse, he was right.' She pulled in a breath. 'There's an awful lot of stuff we don't agree on, but his honesty means I can trust him.'

'I can see how that could be a comfort.'

'He has a real chip on his shoulder about the Funaros—not that that'll be news to you. But he told me about Fina.'

Marguerite stilled.

Audrey soldiered on. 'And Danae.'

Marguerite didn't outwardly flinch, but she sensed her grandmother's tension. 'He had no right to speak about such matters.'

'As I said, we're friends. And friends are honest with one another.'

Marguerite's head rocked back. 'Are you saying that you and I are not friends, Audrey?'

'Absolutely not. But I know how much you want to protect me.' She reached across and covered Marguerite's hand. 'And I can't begin to tell you what that means to me.' With a squeeze, she straightened again, returned to her breakfast. 'I know you all think me naive and soft and vulnerable. And I guess I am naive in many ways, but it doesn't mean I'm weak. I'm far stronger than you all give me credit for.'

'I'm sorry, *mi cara*. It is not that I thought you couldn't deal with the truth. But it is so ugly and I wanted to spare you. I would have told you eventually.'

'I know. But I'm glad to know the truth.'

They ate in silence for a bit. 'Grandmother, I'm really sorry you've suffered so much loss—first your daughter and then your granddaughter. It makes me understand why you've ruled the rest of the family with such an iron fist.'

Marguerite stared at her, opened her mouth, but no sound came out.

'I mean, every time someone else in the family makes a mistake—when there's a divorce, a failed business venture, or some kind of tabloid scandal—it must feel as if another person is going to follow the same path Danae and Fina did.'

'I gave the two of them far too much freedom.' The older woman sighed. 'I do not wish to make the same mistake with anyone else.'

'Their choices weren't your fault, Grandmama. They both had the world at their feet. They should've valued what they had. It's on them, not on anyone else.'

She pretended not to notice when Marguerite dabbed surreptitiously at her eyes. This woman took far too much blame for what had happened when all she'd been trying to do was keep her family safe.

'I have this same argument with Gabriel. He seems to think just because Danae and Fina went off the rails, the rest of the Funaros will go off the rails, too. He takes as his proof various family members' missteps, shortcomings and scandals and says, *"See? They're going the same way."* But that's absurd. All families are complicated, and every person makes mistakes regardless of how rich or poor, famous or obscure they are, and the Funaro family is no different.'

'My word, Audrey.' Marguerite's voice was faint.

She winced in her grandmother's direction. 'Some days we're so immersed in our different projects we barely speak. But other days we seem to—' she shrugged '—cover a lot. And as I told him, he's a member of this family, too, so…'

She trailed off before reaching out to grip her

grandmother's hand. 'I just wanted you to know that I know…about Fina and Danae.' She sent her a smile. 'I don't want you to worry so much about me.'

Marguerite squeezed her hand in reply.

'And to tell you that I trust Gabriel, and that I think you should, too.'

'But he doesn't trust me.'

'If the two of you would just give the other a chance, you'd see each other the way I see the both of you.'

'Well, I'll think upon what you've said. Now, speaking of letting each other into secrets…about this party you're throwing for me…'

She did her best to feign shock. 'Who spilled the beans?'

Marguerite laughed. 'I know exactly what you're up to so don't be coy with me, young lady.'

Audrey had to laugh then, too. 'Okay, so I figured you wouldn't really want to be surprised. But the rest of the family are so enamoured of the idea.'

'Yes, I'm sure they'd love to see me at a disadvantage.'

'You're wrong, you know? This is just giving people a chance to do it the way they want to do it—and in a way they hope will make you happy.'

One imperious eyebrow lifted.

'Okay, well, maybe there's one or two people who are mean-spirited enough to enjoy seeing you at a disadvantage, but families…what are you going to do, huh? We won't give them the satisfaction.'

'May I see the guest list?'

'Absolutely, though I was keeping it small and intimate—no more than fifty people—but I'd love to know if there's anyone else I should include.'

'I'd like to make sure a couple of old school friends are on the list.'

'Also, Lili is in charge of choosing your birthday cake. Now, I can easily sway her away from the ice cream cake she has her heart set on, so if you'd rather a black forest cake or lemon gateaux, now is the time to speak up.'

'My dear granddaughter, I'm sure you'll ensure there's a variety of desserts to cater to every taste. I'm more than happy with whatever Lili chooses.'

'Excellent.' She could tick that off her to-do list. Pulling her hands into her lap, she gripped them tightly. 'Now, on a completely different topic, have you given any more thought to the foundation I'd like to set up in Johanna's name?'

'I'm sorry, Audrey.' Marguerite rose. 'I have a rather important meeting with one of my brokers. We will talk about it later.'

Marguerite swept from the room and Audrey frowned at the pastry on her plate. But later *when*?

'Are Wednesday nights the hotbed of vice you were expecting?'

Audrey trailed her fingers across Gabriel's

chest. She loved the feel of him—the firm smoothness of his skin. She loved touching him after they'd made love. She couldn't explain the sense of peace that stole over her; the warm afterglow and sense of wellbeing.

She'd meant to raise the topic of Wednesday night once they'd boarded the boat. But the moment she'd slipped into the car, he'd sent her such a heated glance that speaking had become impossible, and need and desire took possession of her. The moment they'd closed the studio door behind them, they'd started tearing off each other's clothes, greedy for one another.

He pressed a kiss to the top of her head now. 'Would you like me to apologise?'

'Of course not.' Reaching across, she hugged him hard. 'You should never apologise for having Lili's best interests at heart.'

'But?'

'No buts.' She rested her chin on his chest and glanced up at him. 'Did you enjoy yourself?'

Those stern lips broke into a rare smile. 'I did. As a one-time thing. I prefer sports to romantic comedies and Disney films.'

'And beer to lemonade.'

A laugh rumbled through him. '*Si.*'

'Also, I told Marguerite at breakfast yesterday that I know about Fina and Danae.'

He stiffened.

'I just thought you should know.'

His brow darkened. 'I suppose I should now expect to be called into the headmistress's office for a dressing down.'

'I don't think so. I told Marguerite that I was glad to know the truth and that everyone needed to stop treating me like I might break—that I'm stronger than you all give me credit for. And I told her I trust you and that she should, too.'

His eyes looked like they were going to start from his head.

'She said she'd think about it.' She pressed a kiss to his chest. 'So you need to stop being an idiot and give her a chance.'

'Such lover-like words,' he growled.

She laughed and pressed another kiss to his chest. 'Tell me you'll come to her party.' She kissed her way down his stomach. 'Please?'

'Are you trying to extort an agreement from me?'

She grinned up at him. 'Will that work?'

A laugh rumbled through that powerful frame again, those grey eyes dancing. 'I think it just might.'

'Well, let's see, then, shall we…?'

The day of the party arrived. Livia's car pulled up in the villa's circular drive, and as soon as Audrey saw it, she rushed through to the ballroom where everyone was gathered. Livia and her mother, Caterina, had taken Marguerite to have her hair done—the excuse they'd used to get Marguerite out of the villa so that everyone else could secretly arrive. 'Quiet, everyone, quiet. They're here,' she said, slipping into the room and closing the door behind her.

She took her place at the head of the crowd with Lili, who slipped her hand inside hers. Glancing back behind her, she caught Gabriel's eye. He'd secreted himself at the rear of the crowd. Then Nicolo turned off the lights and smothered them in darkness.

The outside conversation reached them clearly. 'Really, my dear Livia, your birthday is in winter. Surely, you'd prefer a party at the Milan estate.'

'Como is only forty-five minutes from Milan, and the ballroom has such beautiful views over the lake.'

Caterina's voice sounded outside. 'Why don't we just take a look?'

The door opened.

Nicolo snapped on the light.

'Surprise!' Audrey shouted, jumping up and down, grinning madly.

Taking their lead from her, everyone else also started shouting 'Surprise!' and 'Happy birthday!' in Italian and English, and then an unrehearsed but rousing chorus of *'Tanti Auguri a Te,'* the Italian version of 'Happy Birthday,' started up.

To Marguerite's credit, she looked utterly stunned. Though Audrey suspected it wasn't all feigned. Everyone did look ridiculously chuffed and excited. And the ballroom looked fabulously festive with balloons and streamers and tables laden with party food and drinks.

'A birthday party? For me?' Marguerite glanced around with wide eyes, one hand pressed to her chest.

Audrey and Lili danced up to her. 'Tell me you love it,' Audrey said, grinning at her.

'I adore it,' she said, kissing Audrey's cheek. 'Thank you, my dear.'

She said it with such tenderness, Audrey's throat thickened.

Lili hopped from one foot to the other. 'Were you surprised, Nonna? Were you?'

'Absolutely, Lili.' Her cheek was kissed, too. 'I'd have never guessed, not in a million years.'

Marguerite circulated about the room, thanking everyone and clearly enjoying herself. Which, in its turn, made everyone relax and begin to enjoy themselves as well, letting their hair down in a way Audrey hadn't yet seen them do en masse.

Before long, the French doors were opened to the terrace that had been set with an array of cast-iron tables. A game of croquet started up, and the '60s cover band Audrey had hired when she'd discovered Marguerite loved '60s music, started playing at one end of the ballroom.

People ate, chatted, danced. Marguerite exclaimed over her ice cream cake, blew out her candles and then beamed as everyone sang 'Happy Birthday.' It was the perfect party.

'You've danced with just about everyone except me.'

Gabriel's voice had all the fine hairs on Audrey's arms lifting in the most delicious manner. She turned to find him standing behind her, so close she could reach out and trace a finger down his chest.

Don't think of his chest.

'Would you do me the honour?'

Did she dare? They'd avoided each other so far—it had seemed wise. She was afraid that once she was in his arms, they'd give themselves away.

'It occurs to me that if we don't dance, it might look strange…raise questions.'

'Good point.' They didn't want to do that.

What harm can it do?

She allowed him to lead her to the dance floor. The band was currently belting out a Chubby Checker number. They wouldn't be dancing cheek to cheek, thigh to thigh.

Gabriel moved well, which shouldn't surprise her, but it had awareness creeping across the surface of her skin, and her lungs contracting. As if aware of the direction of her thoughts and wanting to break the spell, Gabriel took her hand and spun her around. She couldn't help laughing, and was breathless when the song came to an end. With a pounding heart, she waited for the next song. She'd allow herself the luxury—and exhilaration—of one more dance and then she'd continue with her hostessing duties.

The first notes of the Beatles' classic 'Hey Jude' sounded through the ballroom and she swallowed. Who didn't love this song? But it was a slower number and…

Glancing up from beneath her lashes, her pulse picked up speed as Gabriel's gaze darkened, but without a moment's hesitation, he pulled her into his arms. Everything inside her quickened. He held her closer to him and she allowed her eyelids to droop for just a moment, to relish it and breathe him in. They didn't talk. They just swayed to the music and lived in the moment.

All too soon, the song came to an end.

'Don't look around or get tense, but Marguerite's watching us,' he murmured in her ear. 'I'm going to cut in on Sergei and Paulette and we'll swap partners.'

'Excellent plan.'

They successfully avoided each other for the rest of the party. But the memory of being in his arms had burned itself into her mind. She couldn't wait for Monday to come when the two of them would be alone in his studio once more.

'Gabriel, Audrey…a word, if you don't mind?'

Everything inside Gabriel clenched at the imperious voice located somewhere behind him, but he kept his face bland and disinterested. His usual hostility where Marguerite was concerned was... well, not entirely absent, but certainly diluted.

Audrey's doing. She *had* made him see Marguerite in a different light. He just didn't know if he trusted in it yet or not.

He watched as Lili raced across to hug her great-grandmother before heading to the kitchen with the nanny. In movies and books, children were often used as a kind of barometer to indicate whether someone was good or bad beneath their crusty exterior. He reminded himself that was fiction, and how easily children could be manipulated. But even as he did, he couldn't deny the strength of the bond between his daughter and the older woman.

'Come.' Marguerite led them through several rooms on the ground floor to the library that acted as her unofficial study. She took a seat behind a large oak desk and waved them to the seats on the other side. His every sense went on high alert.

'This feels remarkably formal.'

Audrey voiced his own thoughts as they sat. It was an effort not to reach out and take her hand, to help support her through whatever ordeal was about to come. Because he was in no doubt that some confrontation was about to take place.

Marguerite laid both her hands flat on the desk and drew in a long breath. 'So...the two of you didn't heed the advice I gave to you when Audrey first arrived here.'

Audrey leaned forward. 'You're going to have to be more specific, Grandmother.'

'About the two of you not becoming romantically entangled.'

After one frozen second Audrey sat back again, lips pursed. She glanced at Gabriel. 'You don't lie.'

'No.' Though in this instance he would. If she wanted him to. And *that* realisation sent a strange kind of panic racing through him. He'd sworn to never change for another woman. It only led to heartache and—

'And I don't want to.'

The panic hurtled to a halt. He stared at her as she turned back to Marguerite. 'What gave us away?'

'You're not going to deny it?'

'Absolutely not. I've no desire to lie to you. I know you warned me off him, Grandmama, but…'

He wondered if Audrey was aware of the way her casual *Grandmama* affected Marguerite—the easy affection it indicated. The older woman hid it well, but the word sent a ripple through her every time it was uttered—like a light breeze through the fronds of a massive weeping willow.

He suddenly yearned to capture that image in wood and steel and glass.

He glanced at Audrey. This extraordinary woman waltzed into his life, and after an eight-month drought he was now brimming with inspiration. It made no sense.

'But?' Marguerite prompted.

'The thing is—' Audrey pressed her hands together '—I think you've misjudged Gabriel. And,' she continued, lifting her chin, 'I decided to follow my own instincts where he was concerned.'

Marguerite nodded, though it wasn't in agreement.

'He's not heartless or callous.'

Marguerite had told Audrey he was heartless and callous? He wanted to rail against such an assessment, but he couldn't. In their interactions since Fina had died, his ferocity had been on a tight leash, but at different times he'd allowed the older woman to see it—hoping it would keep her at a distance.

'It was our dance at the party, wasn't it?' Audrey said. 'It gave us away.'

'Does it matter?'

'No, I don't suppose so,' Audrey conceded.

Marguerite sighed. 'It was the way you so assiduously avoided each other at the party. You tell me that you and Gabriel are such good friends, and yet you do your best to not spend any time together when other people are around. It is a realisation that has been playing on my mind since our girls' night. Saturday's party confirmed it.'

'Grandmama…'

That ripple again—tree fronds moving gently in the air.

'Please don't take this the wrong way, but my relationship with Gabriel is nobody's business except his and mine.'

'I'm afraid, my dear, that's where you're wrong. What happens between the two of you has the potential to have a direct bearing on current custody arrangements pertaining to Lili.'

Audrey's jaw dropped.

'For the last two years, Gabriel and I have been walking on eggshells to avoid further unpleasantness. He would rather walk away from this family and would be delighted for Lili to not know any of us. He knows, however, that I would fight that with all the resources at my not inconsiderable disposal. We both know, as well, that such a battle would upset Lili. And we should like to spare her that.'

Audrey glanced from him to her grandmother. The distress in her eyes tore at him. 'We are all adults here,' he found himself saying.

'Fina was an adult, too,' Marguerite shot back. 'And we all know how well that turned out.'

'Fina was a fool,' Audrey said, making both him and Marguerite blink. 'From the little I know, I doubt any of us could consider her a fully functioning adult.'

Marguerite eventually shook herself, shooting

a glare at Gabriel. 'I can't believe you would risk the hard-won equilibrium we have arrived at.'

Audrey gave a soft laugh. 'I'm not sure he had much choice.' Marguerite stared at her. 'Grandmama, you're a woman of the world. Have you never taken...*matters* into your own hands?'

For a moment he thought Marguerite might laugh, but the brief twinkle in her eye darkened again. 'Audrey, it would grieve me greatly to see you hurt.'

'But—'

'You tell me there is a great honesty between you and Gabriel. Does he know, then, that you have fallen in love with him?'

His every muscle stiffened in painful protest. Audrey didn't love him! Love had never been in the cards.

Audrey gaped at her grandmother.

Deny it, he ordered her silently. *Deny it!*

One of Marguerite's hands briefly fluttered to her throat, before it was once again clasped in front of her. 'You do not answer me.'

'I, um...' Audrey moistened her lips, and even through the panic and denial, a shot of desire, hard and dark, speared through him. He still wanted her.

But he didn't want her heart.

'Audrey?' Did that voice belong to him? 'We said...' He swallowed. 'Does Marguerite speak the truth?'

'I…' Her brow furrowed. 'I don't know.'

She didn't know? How…?

He watched her mind race behind those dark eyes, saw the awful realisation filter across her face in a slow, sickening wave. His hands clenched. He wanted to throw his head back and howl.

'Yes.' She swallowed. 'I just didn't realise it until this moment.'

He believed her. With any other woman he'd suspect some hidden agenda—a hope that she could trap him into a permanent arrangement. But not Audrey.

She gave a funny little laugh. *A laugh*. How could she laugh at a time like this?

'I told myself I could control my emotions. I kept telling myself I wouldn't fall in love with you, thinking that would make it true, but—' She broke off, her eyes dark in a pale face. 'Apparently, that's not the way emotions work.'

An ache gripped his chest.

She winced and sent him an apologetic grimace. 'If it's any consolation, I didn't mean to.'

It wasn't any consolation whatsoever!

'You make me feel alive. You make me feel as if I could achieve anything. You're kind and smart and protective of those you care about. You're also demanding, and sometimes moody.'

He blinked.

'You're a generous lover, a fabulous father and…' She shrugged. 'Of course I fell in love with you. How could I not?' She stared down at her hands. 'I guess I didn't want to face the truth because I didn't want what we had to end.'

He rubbed a hand over his face. Of course it had to end, but things inside raised a ruckus at the thought. And the knowledge that he'd hurt her twisted through him in a torturous knot of self-condemnation.

'You want to know what my real mistake was? Thinking that we were like family. That just because I felt at ease with you and because we were honest with one another and because you saw something in my art and seemed to see something in me, that meant you'd stick.'

That he'd...what?

'In the same way that me and Jo and Nonna and Frankie stuck together—there for each other through thick and thin.' She didn't raise her voice, didn't shout and rail at him. 'But that was just wishful thinking.' She shook her head, her eyes narrowed as if the glare of the truth was hard to take. 'I was never special to you.'

'That's not true. You—'

She raised an eyebrow and he bit the rest of his words back. The fact remained that he didn't love her, and to give her false hope would be unkind.

'Gabriel, if you don't want to hurt my granddaughter more than you already have...'

He lifted his head to meet Marguerite's gaze.

'You have to discontinue this affair and walk away.'

She was right. He hated it. But she was right.

Marguerite pulled in a breath. 'Unless you, too, want more?'

'My heart was never on the table.' The words fell from his lips, strangely impassive. Beside him, Audrey flinched. 'We agreed love was not part of the equation.' They'd *promised*! 'You're right, Marguerite. This needs to stop. I have no desire whatsoever to cause pain to Audrey.'

He turned to her. 'Audrey—'

'Oh, God, please don't, Gabriel. I don't want platitudes or sympathy. I already feel foolish enough.'

'You are not a fool!' Hearts had minds of their own. He was the fool for thinking they could keep emotions out of it.

Audrey rose. 'I want to assure you both that I harbour no resentment or ill feeling towards Gabriel. Nothing that has happened between us needs to affect the custody arrangements you have in place for Lili.'

She turned with eyes that were strangely flat— as if the sunshine had been bled from them. Her lips struggled into a smile. His heart burned that it should now be such an effort for her to smile at him.

'I hope you will still allow me to spend time with Lili.'

He rose, too; took her hand. 'Lili loves you. She will look to you in the future. She needs you in her life. I will do everything in my power to safeguard your relationship.'

'Thank you.' She reclaimed her hand and her graveness had a different kind of panic racing through him. Would they no longer be able to share their ideas and challenge each other creatively? Would she no longer chivvy him out of a dark mood or make him see the beauty encased in *everything*? Would they now be so distant from one another that—?

'If you'll both excuse me, I think I'd like a bit of time on my own.'

But it was Monday, and they were supposed to be working at the studio—

With a smothered oath, he crushed that thought. All of it was now at an end, but he couldn't help grieving for what they'd lost.

Audrey stiffened and then whirled on him. 'What do *you* have to swear and be grumpy about? *Your* precious heart's still safe and sound.'

He swallowed. He understood her anger. 'I'm just sorry that—'

'No, you're not. Your world is still the safe little prison it's always been.'

His anger leapt then, too. 'We had a deal!'

'And I broke it.' Her hands slammed to her hips. 'So what? *Deal* with it.'

He gaped.

'Except you won't, will you?' She poked him in the chest. 'You won't do anything, because you're a coward. You'll run away every bit as fast as my mother and father did when things got too hard.'

He clenched his hands so hard, he shook.

'You think loving someone is a prison, but it's not. It can be wonderful and—' She broke off, breathing hard. 'You refuse to try again because it didn't work out with Fina. What kind of attitude is that? Art doesn't work like that, and neither does love or life.'

He opened his mouth, but nothing came out.

'You accuse the Funaros of being profligate, but it's better than being what you are—*a big, fat, emotional miser!* You set your heart against me before you even met me, and nothing that came after was ever going to change that. You said we were friends. You said I was special to you. You told me I was an extraordinary woman, but none of that was enough for you, was it? *Why?* Because biologically I'm a Funaro!'

She was breathing hard, but straightened and looked him dead in the eye. 'As long as your heart remains safe, you don't care how much you hurt anyone else.'

With that, she turned and left.

Everything inside him throbbed. He wanted to yell, chop wood, kick a ball as hard as he could… swim laps until he was exhausted. Anything to rid his body of this awful tension. Instead, he thumped back down to his chair.

Marguerite sighed. 'You're a fool, Gabriel.'

'I deserve something far harsher than *fool*.' Why hadn't he taken more care? Why hadn't he—?

'A fool for letting her go.'

It took a moment for her words to sink in. 'Don't pretend you're not relieved. You warned Audrey off just as you warned Fina off. You've never considered me good enough for this family.'

The older woman rested back, her fingers steepled. 'You have it wrong, my dear.'

He gritted his teeth. He was not her *dear*.

'It was the other way around. I warned Fina off because I knew she was using you as a weapon to make a childish and selfish statement. You were young and idealistic and I knew she would hurt you…lay waste to your dreams.'

His jaw dropped.

'She was such a troubled young woman and I did not know how to help her. Or you. I failed her. Just as I failed her mother. And as I've failed you, too.'

He hauled his jaw back into place, his heart thundering. He recalled all that Audrey had said to him about Fina and straightened. 'You didn't let either one of them down, Marguerite. You gave them both every advantage life had to offer.' Rubbing a hand across his chest, he nodded. 'Audrey is right. They failed themselves, and yet, we continue to bear the brunt of the guilt and regret.' It was time to let it go.

'Audrey is not like Fina.'

No, she was unlike anyone he'd ever met.

'She would not walk all over your heart and treat you as if you were worth nothing.'

'She is kindness personified.'

'And yet, you tell me you do not love her. *That*, my dear Gabriel, is what makes you a fool.'

He gaped at her.

'Go!' She waved an imperious hand at the door. 'I have better things to do than talk with stupid men. I need to ring the girls—'

'The girls,' he parroted.

'Livy, Tori and Ana. We shall rally around Audrey, drink champagne cocktails, eat chocolate and watch some dreadful movie.'

Without him. He was being forced out and the injustice burned through him.

Marguerite glared down her nose at him. 'Broken hearts mend, and we will help Audrey's mend as quickly as possible.' She nodded once, hard. 'We will find her a new prince, and soon you shall be forgotten, and all of this will feel as if it had never happened.'

Everything inside him rebelled at the thought. He shot to his feet, but the words he wanted to shout refused to push past the lump in his throat. Without another word, he strode to the door, but before he slammed through it, he swung back.

'You call me a fool, but you'll be the bigger fool if you don't support Audrey's plan to create a foundation in her sister Johanna's name.' If he could do nothing else, he could at least make Marguerite see sense on this one issue. 'Family means everything to Audrey, but she will not betray her past family to achieve one in the present. If you make her choose, she'll walk away.'

With a heart more broken than he'd left her with. He wanted to throw his head back and howl. Who would she then turn to?

Without another word, he left.

CHAPTER THIRTEEN

AUDREY FLED TO her room, craving sanctuary and quiet, but all too soon the enforced inactivity began to grate. After dragging on her old jeans, she headed outside to the gardens. The estate was large and, if she wished it, she'd be able to avoid bumping into anyone.

She set off for the gardens farthest away from the villa, where no one would be able to spot her from the windows. She walked briefly beside the water, but that didn't help. It simply reminded her of Gabriel's studio.

If Marguerite hadn't called them into the library, she'd be at the studio now. She'd have had a chance to make one more memory to help shore her up on the lonely nights ahead. Because she didn't doubt there'd be long, sleepless nights where the longing for Gabriel would wring her dry and leave her feeling torn and empty.

Turning her back on the extraordinary view, she started down the most beautiful of avenues—tall trees and shrubs towered on either side, making her feel as if she were the only person in the world. But even that brought no comfort.

Finally, she flung herself down in a shady clearing, the scent of wisteria and pine thick in the air. What on earth had she been thinking? Love hadn't been part of the plan.

Falling to her back, she stared up at an impossibly blue sky. She hadn't *wanted* to fall in love. It had been the furthest thing from her mind. For heaven's sake, Gabriel had been more than adamant about his feelings on the subject. It's not like she hadn't been warned.

How could she have been so stupid? So *blindly* stupid?

Pressing palms to hot eyes, she swallowed hard. She'd been so ready to believe they were friends. That what they had meant something to him. *Why?*

Because they'd been honest with each other, had shared a few secrets, had found common ground in their art? None of that had meant he cared for her. Nor did the fact that she'd helped him through his creative block, or that he saw something of value in her fibre art. She was the one who'd thought that'd meant something. Not him.

A growl left her throat. Why had she allowed herself to think it had signified something deep and lasting? Would she never learn?

She'd made that same stupid mistake with Gabriel as she had with her father—seeing something that wasn't there. Gabriel might not have meant to hurt her, but he didn't care for her any more than her father did, in a kind but careless way. As soon as something more was demanded of him, he'd turned tail and fled.

What she hadn't realised was how much loving a man like that would tear her apart.

I'm sorry, but...

A humourless laugh left her lips.

But. It was the story of her life. Gabriel had proved what she'd already known—that she'd never be enough for him. His prejudices, his bitterness, his resentments, were all so much bigger than any feelings he might have for her. And he'd cut off all such feelings at the knees rather than dare feel anything like that for her—*a Funaro.*

But she'd finally learned her lesson. Never again would she waste that much time, energy and effort on a man who'd closed his heart. Her hands clenched. She was tired of not being enough, of being made to feel less than, being made to feel like a fool.

A hard lump stretched her throat into a painful ache. And yet, even now she ached to see him with every breath she took. Even though she knew seeing him would be like torture.

She sat up. Should she leave Lake Como?

Her heart pounded, but her mind grew suddenly clear. To leave would hurt Marguerite and she wouldn't do anything to hurt the older woman. Marguerite had become dear to her. She might not be able to have the man she wanted in her life, but she did have her family. She loved this odd assortment of people who'd come into her life. And there was strength in love, even if Gabriel couldn't see it.

And why on earth should she let him chase her away when she'd found a place to belong? If he chose to remain an outsider, that was his problem not hers.

'Fine.' She hitched her chin at a particularly spectacular pine tree: 'I need to make a new plan.'

Actually, she had the plan Gabriel had created for her for when, as he'd put it, all her hopes and wishes surrounding the family came tumbling down. Except the family *was* everything she'd wished for—that wasn't the part of her life that was tumbling down.

A lump lodged in her throat. Neither she nor Gabriel could have envisaged then that it would be *he* who'd bring her world tumbling down. Because he lacked the courage to love.

Gritting her teeth, she ordered herself to focus on a new plan. First, she'd keep working on her art. She'd ask Marguerite for studio space somewhere on the estate. There must be a garden shed that wasn't in use that she'd be able to co-opt. And she'd take classes somewhere when this summer was over and the family returned to Milan. And she'd contact that agent, too; invite him to take a look at her work. She didn't need Gabriel for any of that.

Oh, but—

She cut that thought dead, pulled out her phone and sent Gabriel an email. She needed to draw a line under all that had gone before.

Gritting her teeth, she thanked him for mentoring her—she was grateful—added a line mumbling some nonsense about remaining friends, and ended with a request for him to let her know when it would be convenient for her to collect her materials.

And just like that, it was over. She swallowed

a sob, dusted off her hands, she set her phone to the ground. One: her family. Two: her art. She'd throw herself with vigour into both.

On cue, her phone pinged. Turning it over, she found a text from Marguerite.

The girls are on their way. Champagne cocktails. Chocolate. Assorted movies at the ready. Anything else?

She had to blink hard as she read the message; acknowledged the love behind it. Gabriel might not love her. Her heart might be broken. But she had a family who cared, and that was something to be grateful for.

She texted back:

Face packs and pizza.

Then she hauled herself to her feet. She refused to wear her oldest, daggiest jeans to this impromptu pity party. She could do better than that.

The moment Gabriel strode into his studio, he knew it had been a mistake to come here. He should've done something else, gone somewhere else. Audrey permeated every inch. From her coffee cup left to drain on the sink, to the container of biscuits she'd baked, to the pile of yarn on one of the workbenches. Lavender scented the air, and the current silence mocked the remembered laughter, the arguments, the earnest discussions about art.

He glanced at the mezzanine and rubbed his hands over his face, his eyes burning. Everything *ached*.

Why the hell couldn't Marguerite have left well enough alone?

Because she didn't want to see Audrey hurt.

He stilled. He didn't want that, either. The knowledge he'd hurt Audrey, even unwittingly, rubbed his soul raw.

He should never have let a Funaro into his studio. He should've realised it'd cause nothing but trouble.

Except Audrey wasn't like the other Funaros. She was warm and friendly and open-minded—

His head lifted. Marguerite hadn't been cold and unfriendly this morning. She'd been concerned. Oh, she'd torn a strip off him for hurting her granddaughter, but that was nothing more than he'd deserved.

The party on Saturday hadn't been cold and unfriendly, either. It'd been fun, a true celebration.

Walking across to *Ties That Bind* and whipping off the dustcover, he stared at it once more. Audrey was a fine artist and the world would soon discover her. But she was a sculptor, too—of people. She dug until she found the good in them and she somehow brought that to the fore so everyone else could see it, too.

Marguerite and her kin hadn't been cold and unfriendly. At least, not in recent times. Maybe the cold and unfriendly one had been him?

The thought made him swallow. Audrey was right. He'd been so determined to ensure another Funaro couldn't take advantage of him that he'd built a wall around himself with huge no-trespassing signs tacked all over it to keep the rest of the family at bay. His hands clenched and unclenched. It wasn't an edifying revelation.

It might've been better for his peace of mind now, but he didn't regret allowing Audrey entry into his sanctuary here. The only thing he regretted was hurting her. He'd move heaven and earth to make that otherwise.

You can.

His temples throbbed and his heart pounded. Wheeling away, he shook his head, but Marguerite's words sounded through his mind.

She's not Fina.

He knew she wasn't Fina! She was ten times the woman Fina was. But there was too much at stake. It wasn't just his heart he'd be risking but Lili's.

You're a fool.

Marguerite's words again, but what did she know? And—

His mouth dried. His heart thundered in his ears. Audrey *wasn't* Fina. If the worst did happen, if a romance between him and Audrey soured, Audrey wouldn't abandon Lili. He felt the truth of that in his bones. In that moment everything inside him yearned towards a future he'd never dared let himself dream about again.

Swinging back to stare at Audrey's artwork, he finally saw it in a new light—her light. The various threads crisscrossing the figure at the centre weren't shackles or restraints. Those threads were in shades of shimmering gold, peacock blue and pale pink. They *weren't* symbolic of the Funaro fortune as he'd previously thought. They were symbolic of family—of attachment, compassion…love.

These weren't ties that bound one against their will. They were the kinds of connections that anchored a person, helped them find their place in the world. These ties created a sanctuary, a safe place… a haven where a person could be themselves.

He glanced around his studio. Audrey's was the real sanctuary, not this place where he'd tried to keep the rest of the world at bay. His studio wasn't a sanctuary; it was a hideaway.

In that moment he agreed with Marguerite— he was a fool. He loved Audrey with every atom of his being; he'd just been too much of a coward to admit it.

His phone vibrated, alerting him to an incoming email. His heart leaped when Audrey's name flashed across the screen. With fingers that shook, he opened the message.

Dear Gabriel,
I'm very grateful for all you've done. Under your expert eye, my technique and artistry have improved a hundredfold. Clearly it is not going

to be viable for me to continue to study under you, given today's revelations, but I very much hope we can remain friends.

Friends? He didn't want to be friends. He wanted them to be lovers. For the rest of time.

If it's not too much trouble, I would appreciate it if you could arrange for my supplies and the pieces I've been working on to be packed up and sent to the villa. Or, if it's more convenient, please let me know a time when I can organise to do so myself.

She was already moving forward with her life—sensible, straightforward, classy. It hit him then how strong Audrey really was. She'd never needed a protector. All of this time, she'd been the warrior fighting for the family she could see beneath all the hurt and bluster and pride.

He lifted his head. It was time to stop hiding. It was time he started fighting for the life he wanted, too. And he wanted Audrey—heart, body and soul. And if he was going to convince her that he truly did love her, that he would do everything in his power to look after her and make her happy, he was going to have to prove it to her.

He stared at her artwork and knew exactly what he had to do.

CHAPTER FOURTEEN

THE BOAT POWERED across the lake with a no-nonsense speed that set Audrey's teeth on edge. She didn't sit in her usual seat. She didn't face forward as she normally would. There was nothing normal about any of this.

It made no sense, but she wanted to rail against the fact that it wasn't Gabriel driving the boat. He'd hired someone to take her across to the studio so she could oversee the packing up of her equipment.

Folding her arms, she glared at the whitewash they left in their wake. He couldn't make his stance any clearer if he'd bellowed it at the top of his lungs from a megaphone. He *didn't* want to see her. He *didn't* want to remain friends.

Jerk!

In a dim part of her mind, she knew he was only trying to save her further pain. A low growl sounded in the back of her throat. Why did everyone think she was going to fall in a heap just because she'd had her heart broken? She wasn't that pitiful.

And not seeing him—having him avoid her as if she'd *betrayed him*—

Closing her eyes, she concentrated on her breathing. The one good thing about today was not being the object of the loving but watchful gazes of Marguerite and the rest of the family. She knew they only wanted to help, but… Yesterday she'd only just managed to stop herself from yelling at everyone to stop watching her.

It will get better. It will get better.

She crossed her fingers.

The boat slowed and bumped to a rest at the tiny dock. She pulled in a breath, girded her loins before disembarking with an ease that had been alien to her two months ago. She glanced at the driver, who cleared his throat and shrugged. 'My instructions were to remain here.'

With a nod, she set off along the path that wound through the trees. The men hired to help her pack were probably already at the studio. As she rounded the curve and topped the rise, though, and the studio came into view, she stuttered to a halt.

Everything that had happened there played through her mind. The disagreements between her and Gabriel, the challenges they'd thrown at each other, the moments when they'd worked together in complete harmony. He'd called her an artist; had given her the permission to explore and experiment; had urged her to dig deeper and discover the heart of the things that moved and interested her. Here her knowledge had deepened and her skills had developed and…

He'd opened up a new world to her.

She refused to think of the other new world he'd opened up to her—a world of sensuality and pleasure and intimacy. Today she'd focus on the future. Not what had been. He'd given her the tools and the contacts to continue to develop her art. *That* was what she'd think about.

That and setting up The Johanna Foundation. This morning Marguerite had called her into the library and had agreed to support Audrey's desire to set up a foundation in Johanna's honour. She'd apologised for her tardiness and had confided her grief at never having had the chance to meet her late granddaughter. 'Whenever I began thinking about how we would set the foundation up and how to make it work, it was... I found it so painful to think about. I so wish I'd had a chance to meet Johanna the way I've had the chance to meet you. I know that I would have loved her, too. So I kept putting it off, kept trying to avoid the grief and regret. I can see now that wasn't fair to you.'

She'd also confided that it was Gabriel who'd convinced her to move forward with Audrey's plan. Apparently, that was something else she ought to feel grateful to him for.

Shaking herself, she continued along the path. Not giving herself a moment to think, she reached for the door, sighing in relief when it opened. That could've been awkward. Gabriel had never given her a key.

'Oh, like that's a surprise,' she muttered under her breath. He'd only ever given her the parts of himself he'd been comfortable sharing.

Her fleeting resentment, though, was no match for the memories that immediately assailed her—none of them to do with embroidery or art of any kind. She stared at the back wall, recalling their first time and how they'd not even fully undressed—too hungry and greedy and wild for each other.

She should have known then. Should have known that to feel so much so soon meant she was already too invested. That it would end in tears.

Shaking the thought off, she faced the room. Nothing stirred. Nobody stood to greet her or awaited instructions.

'Hello?' She moved farther inside, resolutely averting her gaze from the mezzanine level. Now wasn't the time to wallow. She could do that tonight in the privacy of her own room where no one could see.

Her voice echoed in the space, but nothing else moved. Had she misunderstood the message? Maybe she was supposed to pack her things up and leave them for someone to bring back to the villa later. Had Gabriel left a note?

She strode across to the bench where she'd worked, but there was no note there, and then across to the kettle. Nothing. Opening the side door, she glanced out, but nobody sat outside enjoying the view or the sunshine.

It wasn't until she turned back that she saw it—the easel sitting directly in front of the huge wall of glass. A cloth draped over the easel hid the picture, painting, or whatever the artwork was, from view. Was this Gabriel's current project?

Biting her lip, she glanced around. There was nobody to see if she had a peek. Gabriel had never minded sharing his work with her—unfinished or not.

Lifting one corner of the cloth, she glanced beneath... Reefing her hand away, the cloth fell back into place. Her heart pounded.

Was that...*her*?

After glancing around again, she reached out and pulled the cloth completely away to stare at the charcoal drawing encased in a simple wooden frame.

The piece had the same compelling power as his *Maybe* sculpture.

Except this time *she* was the subject. And unlike *Maybe* there was no ambiguity here—no *will she...? won't she...?* questions threaded beneath.

The sketch was of her on the rocks that jutted out into the lake. Where he'd sketched her sitting with her sketchpad all those weeks ago, she now stood, facing the water. Above her, rather than a sun hung a moon, radiating light...somehow bathing everything in the sketch in light.

She took a step closer, trying to work out how he'd done that. The man really was the most extraordinary artist.

The water in this sketch wasn't threatening. All around her it was millpond smooth, though farther out where the light of the moon couldn't quite reach, waves loomed. She took a step back again, her frown deepening. It was as if, because the water farther out wasn't under her influence, it was storm-tossed and restless. Unhappy.

What on earth did it mean?

She pressed a hand to her brow.

If—

She swallowed.

If she saw this picture in an art gallery, and if the woman wasn't her, and if the artist wasn't Gabriel, she'd think the artist had drawn the woman he loved.

But she *was* the woman. And the artist *was* Gabriel.

A footfall sounded behind her and she swung around. *Gabriel.*

Eyes as storm-tossed as the distant waters in his sketch stared at her from a ragged face in dire need of a shave; his hair a thick, tousled mess. He looked how she felt.

For a long moment neither of them moved. He opened his mouth, but she held up a hand and he closed it again. Her heart beat so hard she was sure he must hear it.

Turning to stare at the sketch once more, she forced her spine into straight lines. 'You don't lie?'

'I don't.'

'Then what does that mean?' She gestured at the sketch.

'Many things.'

Exhaustion hit her then. She didn't want to play games. If he didn't want to tell her, fine. Turning away, she made for her bench.

'It means I was wrong about you.'

She stuttered to a halt, but she didn't turn back.

'All of this time you've been telling me that you're strong enough to deal with whatever life throws at you, but I didn't believe you.'

His laugh, full of self-mockery, had her turning.

'I wanted to save you from the same fate as Fina. I couldn't save her, but by God, I'd do my utmost to save you.'

She couldn't move; stood rooted to the spot.

He took a step towards her. 'But it was the rest of us who needed saving. You were right—you are strong, stronger than the rest of us put together. I'm in awe of you, Audrey. You did the impossible—you created a family from practically nothing.'

'Not nothing.' Her voice was low. She tried to strengthen it. 'The framework was there. It just needed…fortifying here and there—the odd wall knocked down and bigger windows to let in the light.'

'You've saved this family.'

The way he said that… Her eyes narrowed. 'Are you now saying *you* feel a part of this family?'

'Yes.'

That was something at least. 'I'm glad.'

'I wanted you to know that I now see how

strong you are.' He gestured at the picture. 'That was one of the reasons for the sketch.'

'Okay.' But while it was a definite compliment, it wasn't a declaration of love. She still wasn't enough for him, and the knowledge burned like acid through her. 'Thank you.' Turning away, she seized a box and started tossing in sketchpads, pencils and yarn.

'I'm out here.'

Holding on to the threads of her temper, she glanced around again. It wasn't his fault he didn't love her. But he had to know that seeing him like this was torture.

He met her gaze—and even with at least twelve feet between them, the intensity of it hit her with the force of a cyclone. His finger pointed to the edges of the sketch where all was dark and storm-tossed. 'I'm here,' he repeated. 'But I want to be here.'

He moved his finger until it was right beside her in the sketch.

'I want to be the innermost person in your circle, Audrey.'

Her heart thundered. 'But you said…' He'd said his heart wasn't on offer. That it had never been on offer.

He moved towards her, those long legs closing the distance between them, his face unreadable.

If he wasn't offering her his heart…? She

slammed her hands to her hips. 'So now you're telling me that you want to be friends?'

He halted in front of her. 'I *don't* want to be your friend.'

She rolled her eyes, knowing she was being contrary but unable to help it. 'Charming.'

'I want to be your lover.'

Her body leapt in instant excitement, but she held it in check. She couldn't do this. Not anymore. 'I want more, Gabriel.'

He shook his head. 'I do not mean in a physical sense.'

She blinked.

'I mean, I do want you in a physical sense—of course I do.' He reached out and took her unresisting hands in his. 'No woman has ever fired my blood the way you do. But I want to be your lover, your *amore*, in every sense of the word.'

She gaped at him, too afraid to hope. She pulled her hands free. 'On Monday you said your heart wasn't on offer and you don't lie and—'

He touched gentle fingers to her lips. 'Clearly, I do lie because I do love you and my heart is yours whether you want it or not.'

The world tilted.

'I lied to you and Marguerite, but only because I was lying to myself. I never wanted to find love again. You were right. It frightened me too much. I told myself one day in the future I would take the plunge again, but—'

He shrugged, his lips twisting as if in disgust. 'I told myself that my affair with you was controllable—pleasurable, but ultimately short-lived—and that it would burn itself out. The thing is, Audrey, it didn't burn itself out. It grew bigger and you became more and more dear to me.'

He was saying... Was he really uttering these beautiful words?

'Marguerite called me a fool when I let you go. Did she tell you that?'

She shook her head.

'It wasn't until you were gone that I realised that she was right.'

'I didn't go anywhere,' she whispered. She'd been mooching about the villa, pining for him.

'But you weren't here!' He gestured around the studio. 'There was no *us*. And I found myself cast adrift.'

She couldn't utter a single word.

'I do not lie, Audrey. I love you.'

Did she dare believe him?

He gestured at the picture. 'I drew that so you could see yourself the way I see you—strong and beautiful and the very heart of your family. I wanted you to know that you *are* enough, Audrey. That anyone lucky enough to have you in their lives is blessed.'

Tears blurred her eyes. The artist *had* drawn the woman he loved. Gabriel *did* love her.

Suddenly, she was in his arms and his hands

were cradling her face and they were kissing each other with a desperate need that had their hips and bodies careening off the furniture.

Seizing her by her upper arms, he dragged her away, his breathing ragged. '*Dio*, I become a beast!'

'I like it when you become a beast,' she panted.

'You undo me.' He tried to frown, but there was a new lightness in his eyes that had her heart lifting. 'At the moment, though, I do not wish to lose control.'

'What a shame.'

He laughed, but sobered again a moment later. 'I love you, Audrey. I love you with all of myself. I know I let you down badly—like your father did, and your mother. I know I hurt you and made you feel less, but I will make it up to you. I swear, if you give me a chance, I will show you how splendidly and perfectly enough you are. I will do all I can to make you love me again. Please tell me I haven't ruined my chance to make amends.'

The lines in his face deepened and he turned grey as if the thought made him physically sick.

Reaching up, she cupped his face. 'I love you with all of myself, too, Gabriel, and I will never let you go. I will always love you and I will always look after you.' She would prove to him that love could be a joy and a wonder and a sanctuary.

As she spoke, the lines in his face eased and the light in his eyes made her heart soar. Holding her gaze with his, he went down on one knee. Her heart crashed about in her chest and her lungs refused to work. 'Gabriel?'

Reaching into his pocket, he pulled out a velvet box. After snapping it open, he held up a ring—a beautifully cut pink diamond that sparkled as the light pouring in at the window caught it. A lump lodged in her throat.

'Now that I know the truth, *carissima*—that I love you—I do not want to leave you in any doubt of my intentions, or what I want for our future. I want you to marry me and be my wife. I want you to be a mother to my daughter. I hope that in time, if you desire it, we can have more children. I want to build a long and happy life with you. I want to dedicate my life to making you happy.'

His outline blurred as tears filled her eyes.

'And just so you know, I sought Marguerite's blessing, too. I did not want to cause any disharmony between you and your grandmother.'

Of course, Marguerite had known what would take place today. She gulped back a happy sob. 'This morning she told me you'd convinced her to pursue the setting up of the foundation in Johanna's honour.'

He rolled his shoulders. 'It was nothing. I simply did not want her making the same mistakes that I had. And I wanted you to have the family you deserve.'

Another sob lodged in her throat, making speech impossible.

He rose, snapping the velvet box closed. 'You do not need to give me your answer now. You can take as much time as you need. I just did not want there to be any misunderstandings or misconceptions. I have been a fool for long enough. I wish to be an open book now and—'

She reached up and pressed her fingers against his lips. 'Gabriel, are you babbling?'

'*Si*. I am very nervous. I love you. This matters a lot to me.'

She pinched herself. This strong, beautiful man really had just gone down on his knee before her. He'd offered her everything he was. Couldn't he see it made her the luckiest woman in the world? 'I would love to marry you. I can't think of anything that would make me happier than to build a life with you and Lili.'

Her words electrified him. 'You mean this?'

'With all my heart.' Reaching up on tiptoe she wrapped her arms around his neck. 'Gabriel, you have the kindest heart and the most honest soul of any person I've ever met. You make me feel seen and known…and loved. I've never felt more alive in my life than I have here in the studio with you. I know how badly your experience with Fina hurt you, but you've found the courage to love again. You're the most wonderful man I've ever met.'

He kissed her then. Warm, firm lips moved over

hers, telling her how much he loved and desired her, how she, too, had brought him alive, opening up a world he'd never imagined. He kissed her until she became boneless with need and drunk on the taste of him. He kissed her with the wildness that she loved.

Lifting her head, she stared into his eyes. 'Is it okay if we lose control now?'

She gasped when he lifted her into his arms and strode towards the staircase. 'Your wish is my command,' he said, grinning down at her.

'Hmm...' She cocked her head to one side and pretended to consider his words as he carried her up the stairs. 'Aren't you being just a teensy bit derivative with that line?'

But then he did something wholly original with his tongue and his hands, and her pulse skyrocketed. 'Okay, scrap that. My mistake.'

Laughing, they fell down to the bed together into a future filled with love and laughter and family.

EPILOGUE

The following summer

DRAGGING A DEEP BREATH into her lungs, Audrey cast one last glance in the mirror before exiting the bedroom she'd been allocated. The excited voices coming from the direction of the living room told her the bridesmaids were ready. Instead of turning towards them, though, she moved down the hall to knock on the door of the master suite. 'Frankie? It's me.'

Frankie threw the door open and they stared at each other in open-mouthed amazement, before Frankie grabbed her hand and hauled her into her bedroom and closed the door.

'You look—' They both started at the same time and then laughed.

Neither she nor Frankie had ever dreamed of a big white church wedding where they wore dresses that weighed almost as much as they did. Their dream wedding had always been much simpler—a garden wedding surrounded only by the people they loved.

'Frankie, you look perfect.' And her cousin did. She'd chosen a boho-inspired ankle-length wedding dress with peekaboo lace and intricate embroidery. The V-neckline was playful and sexy and the pink toenails peeping from their pretty sandals made her smile. 'The most beautiful bride that ever was.'

Frankie laughed. 'I love my dress, Audrey, but I think you might win the honours for most beautiful bride.'

Wrapping an arm around each other's waists, they turned to stare into Frankie's full-length mirror. 'I love my dress, too,' she confessed. The sweetheart neckline, lace bodice and A-line skirt in a soft tulle that floated about her calves were more traditional, and they made her feel like a fairy-tale princess. 'I feel like Cinderella.' She swung to Frankie. 'I'm so glad we're having a double wedding.'

Frankie's eyes sparkled. 'We embarked on this adventure together, Audrey. It's only fitting we now walk down the aisle together as brides. I can't believe it's ended so *wonderfully*. Who knew that one summer could change everything? And this—' she gestured at the two of them '—is the best happy-ever-after possible.'

Audrey's grin widened. Marguerite would probably sigh and shake her head at her granddaughter's inability to contain her happiness, but secretly she knew her grandmother loved that about her. 'I wonder if Nonna knew we'd find our destinies here.'

Frankie shook her head. 'I think she wanted to give us the opportunity to take stock of our lives and decide what was important to us…to help us choose the path that would make us happiest. But not even she could foresee how momentous this summer would prove to be.'

It had been the best gift she'd ever received. 'And are you truly happy with the path you've chosen, Frankie?'

Frankie had recently finished her medical specialty, and when she returned from her honeymoon in Venice, she'd start practising as a family doctor in the nearby village. It was a far cry from her old dream of becoming a neurosurgeon.

Frankie squeezed both of Audrey's hands. 'Totally happy, Audrey, I promise. I know it seems like an abrupt about-face, but this is the right fit for me. And I love Dante with all of my heart. Marrying him… It makes my heart sing.'

Audrey could relate to that 100 percent.

'And I don't have to ask if you're happy. I can see it shining from every pore. Gabriel is a lucky man.'

And she was the luckiest woman alive. Gabriel was everything she could hope for in a husband.

Frankie gave an excited shimmer. 'Are you ready to marry the man of your dreams?'

'I've never been readier for anything in my entire life.'

Not a single cloud marred the blue of the sky on the short drive to the vineyard where their guests—*and grooms*—waited for them. The terrace of Dante's restaurant Lorenzo's had been transformed into a fairyland with flowers and fairy lights, and Audrey and Frankie stood beneath an arbour of flowers at one end of the aisle, smiling guests seated in front of them. At the other end of the aisle against a glorious backdrop of golden hills, green grapevines and a stunning sunset, their grooms waited for them.

Lili looked enchanting as their flower girl, and Dante's sisters looked gorgeous as the bridesmaids in their identical dresses, each in a different pastel shade—Maria in rose, Sofia in peach, and Giorgia in mauve. The small crowd oohed and ahhed as the attendants moved down the aisle, and both Aunt Deidre and Dante's mother, Ginevra, began dabbing at their eyes with handkerchiefs. Even her father looked suddenly emotional and proud. Marguerite might not have a tear in her eyes, but her smile was so large it made Audrey want to sing.

Frankie held out her hand, Audrey took it and they walked each other down the aisle. They'd been each other's main support for as long as they could remember, and it only seemed fitting they should support each other now and walk boldly into their new futures together.

Despite the beauty of the setting, despite being surrounded by all the people she loved, Audrey only had eyes for one person—Gabriel. Those grey eyes never left hers as she moved towards him. Her pulse fluttered with appreciation at the way he filled out his tuxedo—but it was the expression in his eyes that held her spellbound. The desire, the possessiveness, made her skin tighten, but it was the love in his eyes that made her heart pound. For this man she was *enough*. For this man she would *always* be enough.

As they made their vows, their voices rang out sure and true.

When the celebrant pronounced them husband and wife, and told the grooms they could kiss their brides, Gabriel kissed her with such fierce conviction it stole her breath. 'I love you,' he murmured.

'I love you,' she murmured back.

He pressed a warm kiss into the palm of her hand. 'You are beautiful.'

He made her feel beautiful.

Much later, after a glorious dinner, and the cakes had been cut and the bridal waltzes had been waltzed, Gabriel whisked her off to a far corner of the terrace where a huge urn filled with roses hid them from view and pulled her into his arms to kiss her. 'I have been dying to get you to myself.'

Breathless, she reached up to touch his face. 'Happy, Gabriel?'

'*Si*. More than I ever thought possible. Loving you, Audrey, has done what I never thought possible.' He took her hand and placed it over his heart. 'You have healed my heart. I mean to cherish you every single day of our lives together. And you, *cara*? Are you happy?'

'I'm so happy there aren't words—in either English or Italian—to describe it.'

His grin made her heart soar. 'And are you still happy with our honeymoon plans?'

'Yes!'

They'd bought a beautiful old villa on the outskirts of Bellagio that had a gorgeous view of Lake Como and the surrounding mountains. The sale had only gone through last week, and on the spur of the moment they'd cancelled their honeymoon plans to spend it there. Alone. Everyone else still thought they were going to Paris.

The villa was in need of some updating, but that gave them the opportunity to make it truly their own. What's more it had a huge barn they had plans to convert into a joint studio, which might have to take precedence if they were to be ready for their joint exhibition in the autumn. Audrey still couldn't believe the acclaim her work was starting to garner.

'You will not miss the romance of Paris?'

She wound her arms around his neck. 'I can't think of anything more romantic than spending the first week of married life in our new home and truly making it our own. Besides, you have never been away from Lili for a whole week before, and while I know Marguerite has lots of exciting plans to keep her busy, we want to be near at hand in case she should need us.'

Lili's excitement that Audrey was her new mother knew no bounds, but that didn't mean there wouldn't be teething problems. Audrey wanted to make the transition as smooth for her as possible. It was the reason they'd waited a whole year to marry.

'Maybe we can spend our first anniversary in Paris,' she said.

'You are a remarkable woman, Audrey. Do you know that?' He kissed her long and deep, and when he lifted his head, she had to cling to him to remain upright. 'What do you say to leaving for our honeymoon right now?'

Reaching up, she kissed him. 'I think that's an excellent plan.'

* * * * *

If you missed the previous story in the
One Summer in Italy duet
then check out

Unbuttoning the Tuscan Tycoon

And if you enjoyed this story, check out
these other great reads from
Michelle Douglas

Reclusive Millionaire's Mistletoe Miracle
Wedding Date in Malaysia
Escape with Her Greek Tycoon

All available now!